RIPTIDE

RIPTIDE

ELLA THORP ELLIS

drawings by Joel Snyder

Atheneum   1969   New York

c,1
y

FOR STEVE

— BL OCT 7 - '69

CONTENTS

RIPTIDE

THE
MISUNDERSTANDING

IT WAS late afternoon and the wind was rising so that it was necessary to burrow down into the sand to escape it, but still the boys lay on the California beach, huddled together in a semicircle facing the ocean, soaking in the last of the unusual November sun. The wind swept on over them and grabbed hold of the big live dunes rising behind, erupting the tawny sand. Now, with the high tide, the dunes were set back from the ocean only a hundred yards and if the wind shifted slightly the boys would be driven off by the sand. They knew this, but they also felt that this

3

might be the last good day before winter closed in, and so they stayed.

Mike Lamon stood up and the wind battered his lanky body as he moved toward a line of brightly colored surf boards. He was over six feet, tall for fifteen, and he moved a little jerkily as if his size was unfamiliar to him. He chose a flaking fading yellow board and lifted it to his shoulders, balanced a moment, and then started toward the water. He heard someone call after him but did not turn around.

"I don't give a damn. I just don't give a damn," he said aloud, though he was alone. "They can have their secrets. Who cares?"

Mike thought bitterly that it had been a bad day from the start, one of those days when he rubbed every single person he met the wrong way. He should have stayed in bed. This business of Pat's friends giving him the cold shoulder was just the last straw. His brother's crowd were all in college and he was only a Sophomore in high school, but he'd been coming to the beach with them for years. Normally he wasn't the only kid brother along but today it happened that he was. He'd gone surfing, which he preferred to do alone, and they had stayed on the beach and gossiped. Pat was afraid of the ocean, and most of his friends were too lazy to swim or surf.

Maybe it was all just coincidence, but he'd been lying there half-asleep and wishing he had a wet suit so fall surfing wouldn't be like breaking ice when

4

suddenly all talk stopped. He looked around and everyone was looking as if something terrible had happened, and no one said a word. Paul, who had been first string fullback on the football team last year, and whose place Mike had this year, stood up and shook out his towel. He had a funny look on his face, as if he might be coming down with flu.

"Did you say something to me, Paul?" Mike had asked, because he *did* have a disastrous habit of not hearing people. Some guys thought he had a big head because he was on the varsity football squad as a Sophomore, but he just didn't hear. Maybe he was going deaf.

"Nothing to do with you, kid. Relax. Just shoving off, is all. Take care all," Paul had said and walked off. Just like that. And nobody had said one word. Not one. And no one had looked at him. Even Pat had avoided his eyes. Even Pat didn't want him to know what it was all about. Therefore, the hell with them. It was plainly time to take a ride even if the ocean was cold enough to freeze.

He'd already fought with Dad. Not fought so much as gotten the ultimatum. No motorcycle. Granted Dad *had* warned him that he couldn't have wheels until he was sixteen and had driver education, driver training, and a license. And even then it couldn't be a cycle, nasty old cycle. But, the State of California law stated that at fifteen and a half a man could own and operate a motorcycle if he had a permit to drive. He was getting the permit Monday.

So Dad *had* warned him two years ago, but he'd still let him work like a fool for two solid summers picking beans and apricots, knowing that every dime was for a cycle. That had been no secret. He'd saved the six hundred dollars dime by dime, and Dad had let him, never letting out a peep. He'd gone without a new surfboard and a wet suit and everything else he'd wanted for two years. His room was literally papered with pictures of Hondas. Then to get the ax this morning. It was too much. Too much.

It was all very well for Pat to say that the motorcycle was a masculinity symbol he didn't need. How the hell did Pat know what he needed? Pat seldom remembered yesterday, so how could he recall what life was like at fifteen? It *would* be nice, however, to think that another four years would fit him together like Pat, but it wasn't likely. He was already taller, just as four years ago Pat was already a muscle man. When you thought about it, everything about them was contradictory. Pat was the world's laziest man and looked like one of those Greek God statues. Mike was the big athlete and what good did it do? He still looked like a skeleton propped up temporarily for Halloween. Pat was a deeply tanned redhead, and he was a perenially peeling blonde. Only their eyes were alike. Sailor's blue eyes. But even this was a fraud. He loved the sea, and Pat had nightmares that it was a terrible green octopus reaching out to gather him in.

This wasn't putting Pat down. He *had* offered to teach him to drive, after all. Not that it looked like he'd get a chance. Not after Dad's gentle little parting shot.

"Watch it, kid," he'd said. "You're getting to be just about the cockiest rooster this side of the slaughterhouse." Love thy father? Forget it!

Mike stopped just above the high tide line and scanned both the beach and water carefully. This was a boomerang-shaped beach, maybe a dozen miles long. A strip of dunes separated the ocean from the rich truck farming valley where he'd always lived and above the valley rose a broad purple mesa. A hundred years before warlike Indians from that mesa had come roaring down through the valley and over the dunes and slaughtered the lazy peaceful Chumash Indians who lived there and whose shell mounds Mike saw now as he scanned the dunes for some hint as to how fast the wind was rising. He heard the whistle of the 4 P.M. mail train shriek above the pounding surf. You could time the wind by that train, all right. And it wasn't too bad yet.

There was a nasty riptide, though. He watched the clashing breakers critically. Tricky. But he sure wasn't turning back now. Besides, look at that angle. He watched the wave crest and curl, unwinding slowly. A good surfer could catch that crest and ride one of those waves for at least a minute, maybe more. It was breaking like a dream, never mind the rips.

7

Mike knew he'd feel better if he could ride in a couple of good waves. If he could just get unplugged for a while.

It had always been that way. It used to be that when life got too much for him, he'd come down and dig clams. Mom still called clam chowder "Mike's mad stew." But surfing was better, demanded more, demanded absolute attention. And this was a make or break surf if there'd ever been one. The sandy ocean bottom sloped gradually and this made for a long shallow wave that an experienced surfer could ride forever and a hacker could wipe out on ten times out of ten. Just stay clear of the riptides.

He pushed the board through the first line of breakers to the clear water, and it cut cleanly, leaving a wake. The water was cold, and he dunked himself to keep from turning around and heading back to the beach. He wanted to slide onto the board, but the water was still shallow and cluttered with great families of seaweed so he waded, pushing the board alongside him like an old tire.

November was a bad month for seaweed. Always had been. But it was also the month when the seals started back down the coast, and maybe he'd have some for company out beyond the breakers. There didn't seem to be anything so far but a school of small silver perch darting out of range in unison, as if they had one body. He watched carefully for jellyfish because their sting made him swell.

It was deep enough now, but it hadn't gotten any warmer. He'd have a wet suit if Dad hadn't let him save for the motorcycle he couldn't have. Mike lay flat on his board and paddled through the second line of breakers. It was the swells he was after. The wave was useless after it broke. Normally he would sit astride the board waiting for a good swell. When it was sunny the wait wasn't bad because there were always fish or birds to watch. But today was something else. In half an hour the wind would be not only cold but dangerous. He lay flat in a vain effort to get warm. The wind already rippled little eddies across the surface and it was hard to get the feel of a swell. There wasn't another surfer as far as he could see.

Mike missed three or four waves that would have been all right before he felt a proper swell. He could see it building up, beautifully formed, with a curl bending over the top. Then he rose to his knees, crouched, and started paddling. This one should be a beauty.

Rising slowly, he stood and angled toward the front of the board, balancing carefully, feeling the balance fit itself under the curve of the powerfully swelling wave, fearing and knowing it was too late for fear.

Did he have it? He was on! He leaned in toward the wave when he felt the board sliding down. Balance. Easy. Coax it, turn with it, now down. He felt himself suddenly sucked into a vortex and he crouched to meet it, to slide inside the wave, letting it carry him

9

and the board.

Instinct took over now. Mike and the board worked with the curl of the wave, sensing its direction, leaning with it. He moved slightly forward to get more wave under the back of the board. The board should hiss waiting for the strange hush, the roar as it skimmed the edge of the wave. It was warm and dry and a minute could be forever.

But it wasn't going that way. Maybe it was going to be too small. The crazy curl swung back up to the shoulder of the wave. Mike felt the board shift and rose to meet it. He knew he'd had it. There was nothing he could do. But he rose anyhow, leaning toward the wave. Maybe he could still hitch an angle ride. Then the wave caught up with him. The full force of the wave smacked hard, and he catapulted over and over down through the churning darkness, somersaulting inside the turbulence, letting himself go under the breaking wave. He wondered vaguely where his board might be and checked to see if anything was broken. Arms and legs seemed O.K. Just roll with it and wait. Stay down until you are sure the board has landed somewhere and won't land on you.

The bubbly turbulence lightened and he was ready to break the surface. Just a few seconds more. Stay down. Just a little peek now. Nothing to be afraid of. One more little wipe out. Nothing when you've wiped out so many times. A wipe out was no longer even countable, but normal, a normal part of the pleasure of surfing. Just make like a drifting sea anemone. Never fight the ocean because it's bigger.

But he'd need a breath soon. There was no shadow of the board over him but you *could* hit your board and come back with a ten stitcher when you didn't see a shadow. Just wait another little minute to be dead sure that board came down somewhere, somewhere else.

Mike stuck his head out into the air gingerly, saw the surfboard at least twenty feet away bobbing in the wake of the wave and only then worried about the oncoming wave. There was plenty of time to glide easily over the swell.

After the swell he struck out slowly in the general direction of the yellow board. There was no hurry. He felt easy and relaxed and warm. If only the salt weren't so heavy, it would be almost perfect. His eyes burned and his nose was running but that was all right.

Down beach he could see the group of familiar bodies still lying in the same semicircle; blotches of primary colors, stretches of brown, and long square beach towels. There were fewer of them. Only the hardiest and those who always tried to avoid going home were still there. It didn't seem to matter so much anymore if they had a secret. So why did he have to know everything in the world anyway? What did matter was that he'd drifted a long way in the current

11

and it was going to be a long walk back. That board was going to get mighty heavy.

He only gradually became aware of another swimmer nearby. Could be a seal? With a red head? Hardly. Whoever or whatever it was appeared to bounce across the water like an empty box. If it wasn't impossible, he'd say it was Pat. But that was impossible because of all things on the face of the earth, Pat hated and feared the ocean most. Nevertheless it *must* be Pat, and he was sure as heck in trouble! What looked like bobbing was Pat going down and then dragging himself back to the surface.

"Hang on, Pat! Hang on!" Mike swam toward him desperately, using an overhand stroke because it was not only fast but allowed him to keep an eye on his brother.

He took a quick look toward shore. No one on the beach had noticed that Pat was in trouble. No use to yell for help now. No *wonder* people drowned a hundred yards offshore. His surfboard was heading in toward shore. Maybe they'd look out when someone caught that. Couldn't count on it, though.

"I'm coming! Hang on!" Could Pat hear him? Why hadn't he yelled for help? Why didn't he tread water and rest for a while? What on earth was he doing out without a board, anyhow? It took a good swimmer to manage the rips and even the current, and Pat was hardly capable of doing the length of a pool. Oh, oh. Where was he? There he was.

"Hang on! Just a few more seconds, Pat. Tread water! Tread water! Like a dog, just make like a dog!"

"Mike? Mike. Thank God, you're safe!" Pat yelled and went under again. He bobbed to the surface and started treading.

"Thank God I'm all right?" Mike answered. What the hell was he talking about? Unless—unless the crazy wonderful fool was coming out to make some sort of rescue! Pat rescuing *him?* Talk about Don Quixote. Windmills. Waves. Afraid, always afraid of the green octopus of the sea. Oh, it was too much, too much. What a crazy fool, what a wonderful guy! Pat was just the end. Coming all this way out to rescue a brother when he couldn't swim.

"Hang on, man," Mike yelled automatically.

"I'm drowning!"

"Paddle. Or turn over on your back and float. Float!"

Pat turned over on his back and floated. Mike could see that his eyes were closed tight. He couldn't quite reach him, though. Every time he almost made it, the current pulled Pat a little farther out. Don't fight it, the life saving instructor always said. Go around. But there wasn't time. There just wasn't time. He was gaining. Slow and easy. Keep at an angle and never take your eyes off the victim for an instant. He could hear the flat midwestern twang of his instructor. If the victim is panicky, it is better to take him from

13

behind and sling your arm down across his chest, grabbing him under the armpit, than it is to attempt a chin grip. Remember, it is essential to remain behind the victim so that you will not be knocked out by his flailing arms. Crazy old man, let's hope you're right, Mike thought as he finally reached for his brother.

"It's O.K. I can take you in easy, Pat. I'm here now," Mike said as he angled around behind and reached out. He grabbed suddenly before Pat had a chance to strike, talking all the time. "O.K. now, easy does it. Go to sleep, just go to sleep."

Pat jerked violently, muttering incoherently. Mike held tight, wondering if he'd have to knock him out.

"Pat, don't make me sock you," he pleaded.

"Octopus. Octopus. What? Mike?"

"I mean it, Pat. I'll floor you if you don't cut it out. That's better," Mike said gently, letting the current carry them down beach but stroking ever closer to the shore. Keep talking to the victim if you can, the old teacher had said.

"Pat, I see ducks diving into a school of silver fish. A pelican just got his dinner. Big fish. We're going around this clump of seaweed, just dumb old seaweed, and then we hit clear water, just like swimming in a pool. And there's only one little line of breakers after that. Just relax, go limp, please, Pat. O.K., I see some of the gang standing up now. Going home. Haven't seen us." Mike was gulping water, but he tried to keep a soothing monotone. Pat was as heavy now as if he'd passed out. But his eyes were open. Glassy.

"We won't make it," Pat said quietly.

"Shut up!" Mike replied harshly. He could hardly see the people on shore now. The two of them had drifted a long way. But they *were* making it toward shore. Another few strokes and they'd be into the breakers. Another minute or two and Mike would be able to touch bottom, should be able to touch bottom. Better not try until he was sure. You could panic if you tried for the bottom and couldn't touch. He was so tired, but he must hang onto Pat and he must keep swimming. Slow and easy. Make each stroke count. Just four more breakers. Three more. Two more. The last one. The last one. Pat was so limp. Couldn't he help, even now? When Mike finally put his feet down, he was only waist-deep in water.

"Stand up," he said, letting Pat go.

"Thanks," Pat said. They stood leaning on each other, stumbling toward shore.

Mike found the broken clam shells and the seaweed in the frothy shallow water almost unbearably annoying as he lurched toward the dry sand. And the wind must be blowing fifty miles an hour. God, but it was cold. They were probably at least half a mile from dry towels and sweatshirts. They'd have to rest first. Rest in this wind?

"Thanks," Pat said again as they sank into the dry sand and tried to burrow under to where it might still be warm.

Mike shrugged. He was a little embarrassed. After all, Pat had come out in the first place to save *him* from drowning. It took considerably more courage if you couldn't swim and were afraid than if you just happened to be tooling around out there. But, as usual, he couldn't seem to find the right words to tell Pat how he felt.

"I guess I've got claustrophobia, really got it," Pat said softly.

"I thought you were a seal at first, a red-headed seal. But then I got to thinking seals don't have red hair." Mike laughed, and Pat laughed too.

"Say, what were you doing out there, anyhow? I wipe out all the time and you've never turned hero before."

"You've never gone running off without saying a word before, either," Pat reminded him.

Mike remembered guiltily that he'd heard Pat call after him. He'd been mad and hadn't answered. There'd been a lot of water over the dam since then, and it didn't seem important anymore. Better say something, though.

"I thought you had some secret I was too little to hear, so I decided the hell with you all. On top of my fight with Dad, it was just too much. So I went for a ride. Sorry, Pat."

"I'd forgotten to warn you. Paul's gotten his draft notice. He reports to Fort Ord tomorrow at noon.

He had some crazy idea he wanted one last day on the beach the way it always was. No good-byes. You know, pretend there's no draft."

"Oh."

"Look, Mike, he figures maybe he'll come back a basket case. Maybe we all will. So Paul wanted to remember the beach just the way it was. O.K.?"

"Sure." Mike knew Pat was fighting a losing battle to keep his grades up so he wouldn't be draft bait, but that was mainly because it was two years out of his life for nothing—wasn't it? "Do you all feel that way?" he asked.

"More or less. Say, that sun's almost down, and we'll be deep frozen if we stay much longer. I'll race you to the towels," Pat said, standing up and brushing sand off his arms.

"Sure. I'd like to ask you about the draft sometime, though. O.K.?"

"Sometime when my goose pimples don't have goose pimples."

Pat started off at a jog, and Mike followed reluctantly. It was cold, but the wind was dropping now as it often did at sunset, and the sky was gathering color, though the sun still hung out over the horizon. Funny how black the sea always looked at sunset, like some ship had sprayed oil. The gulls and the pelicans and sandpipers were screaming at each other as they dove and dug and scratched for their dinners.

What was the big hurry? Mike ached in every bone. All very well for Pat to go tearing up the beach like a bat out of hell. All he'd had to do was lie still and get pulled in from the water; but if he'd wiped out and then hauled in a flapping ton of lead, he wouldn't be doing the big track and field act either. Nevertheless, Mike strained for a burst of speed. Pat wasn't supposed to know how to run. He'd never live it down if Pat beat him.

Suddenly he stopped. What was that? Mike looked up, and a horn sounded again. There was a green Manx beach buggy on the crest of the first line of dunes. It cruised along the lip of the dunes and then charged straight down the sand toward them like a buffalo.

"Hey! Hold it!" Pat yelled, semaphoring with his hands so they'd see him in time to stop. The buggy swerved by and screeched to a sand spraying stop beside Pat. An old man tanned the color of leather and with a great shock of white hair that fanned out from a bald spot on the top of his head drove the car, and a young girl about Mike's age sat next to him. She had dark curly hair and brown eyes and rosy cheeks. She was laughing at them, and she looked familiar.

"Want a lift, Pat?" The old man said.

Trust Pat to know everyone, Mike thought, as he made a final spurt to catch up with them.

"We sure do! Even my goose pimples have pimples

and our towels and boards and my car are way up the beach. Thanks a lot, Mr. Varian. By the way, this is my brother, Mike. Mr. Varian lives across from where I work at the motorcycle rental joint. I guess you know his granddaughter, Mary."

"Yeah, sure. Hi, Mary. Glad to know you, Mr. Varian, especially right now." Mike smiled. She was the new girl in his class, the one whose parents were in Iran. He'd seen her around the halls and hadn't particularly noticed, but now he couldn't stop looking at her. It wasn't only that she was pretty and stacked, although she was. It was that she was so alive. He felt battered by comparison. It was exhausting just to look at such energy. Of course, today had been one of his more battering days, between Dad's ultimatum against cycles, the wipe out, Pat's misguided heroism, and Paul getting drafted. He wasn't at his best.

"So you're Pat's smart brother? Hear that you want to buy a motorcycle. Shows good sense. I want one myself," Mr. Varian said as Mike and Pat clambered into the back seat.

"Grandpa, you do not!" Mary said emphatically.

Mike nearly fell asleep as soon as he got in the car. Mr. Varian wrapped blankets around them, and being warm was almost too much for him. Dimly he heard Mr. Varian and his brother talking. Mike did not even try to follow their conversation.

He concentrated on the car to keep himself awake. He would have liked to watch Mary, but he could only see the back of her head and that wasn't enough. Besides, he'd never been in one of these Meyer Manx jobs before. Most of the kids used jeeps turned buggy because they were good for competition driving, but this rode a lot smoother. Pat called Manxes popcorn machines because they bounced down the pier past the cycle rental shop where he worked Saturdays without ever seeming to hit the ground. Peculiar looking. This one looked like a turtle on wheels.

They were basically Volkswagens with a shortened wheelbase. Some guys just bought an old Volks, had it shortened, and then lifted off the bodies themselves and dropped this turtle-shaped fiber glass body on the chassis. This one looked like the old guy bought it this way new, though. Everything matched. Even the wide tires looked as if they belonged. And it had all the standard equipment to make it legal for highway driving, too. Fenders, a windshield, windows, lights. No one would have bothered to put all *that* stuff on. It was a cool car all right, and he must be one cool old man to own it.

"Hey, Mike, come to. Mr. Varian wants to sell this buggy and buy a cycle. He's only asking $600."

"Fantastic," Mike said. "It must have a cracked block and a rotten transmission if you're that low. Can't be more than three or four years old." Mr. Varian would know he was kidding.

"It's gotten use all right, but nothing major's wrong that I know. I've used the buggy prospecting, and I don't want to sell high and then worry that some kid's waiting for me with a shotgun." Mr. Varian laughed.

"Grandpa. you are *not* selling this car, and that is final!" Mary said furiously.

"Sometimes you might wonder who is the guardian around here," Mr. Varian said firmly. "I don't have many years left to do what I want, Mary. Therefore, I shall."

"Bet I could get Dad to let you buy this car, Mike," Pat said quietly.

"Ho. Ho!" Mike replied bitterly. Pat must be out of his mind. Besides, he wanted a motorcycle and not a turtle on wheels. Anyhow, it was impossible. They stopped by Pat's car, and Mike opened the door to get out. He hated to unwrap the warm blanket, but he couldn't sit there forever.

"O.K., thanks for the ride. See you, Mary," Mike said, trying not to notice that she had tears in her eyes and didn't reply.

"If anything works out, I'll give you a call, Mr. V.," Pat yelled back as they left.

"Sure, bring your father for a drive, Pat."

"That'll be the day," Mike said, thinking that he would settle for about fourteen hours sleep. All he needed was another scene. This day had already been too much, just too much.

TRIAL RUN

MIKE FELT he'd spent the whole night somersaulting through water, over and over and over. Whenever he came up for air, the surfboard was falling right on top of him. Only, instead of a surfboard it always turned out to be Pat.

Not that he'd gotten much sleep. God knew how, but Pat had persuaded Dad to go for a ride in the dune buggy and to agree "in principle" to the possibility of buying it. Everyone knew there was bound to be something that wouldn't pass Dad's inspection in any car, and especially a dune runner that only cost $600. Still, it did leave Mike with the problem of whether he wanted to spend the only $600 he'd ever earned on that buggy. It was one thing to save it dime by dime for a motorcycle he'd wanted all his life and another to plunk it down for a car he'd never considered. Of course, that was the way Pat operated, but it wasn't his way. He liked to think things out and plan. And of course Dad's little two hour lecture on how much it cost to keep up and run a car didn't help make the decision.

Nevertheless, there they were in Dad's Oldsmobile on the way to Mr. Varian's house. Mary would probably greet them with a shotgun. At least it was a clear day. There weren't more than twenty days in the year when it wasn't foggy until nearly noon along their stretch of the coast. The sun should make Dad feel good because a long stretch of bad weather always reminded him that choosing this "godforsaken stretch of California Arctic" was just more evidence of his lack of judgment if not dementia. Personally, Mike felt that coming *here* to teach history, if Dad *had* to teach history, was the best thing he had ever done.

If only he could remember what the car looked like, maybe he wouldn't feel as if Pat was selling him a bill of goods. Like a green turtle on wheels? All he could see was a turtle and not a car. He'd wanted a cycle because you could roar along the tide line and the wind ripped through your body and you were a part of it all. Could you do that with a car? At least you could probably come closer with a dune buggy than other cars, and the cycle was out, out, out.

There was only one street from town to the beach cabin where Mr. Varian and Mary lived. Mike had walked the road, ridden his bike around its holes, and then walked it again when he was too old for a bike and too young for a motorcycle, nearly every day as long as he could remember. Not many streets, even in beach towns, were made up of seventeen bars, two grocery stores, a firehouse, a barber shop, and one hotel so ratty and run down that it was usually empty in spite of being the only hotel. It was Sunday morning and too early for church, so only a few old men were out, and the street somehow looked weather-beaten and lonely, like a ghost town.

Mike was glad when they crossed the high bridge running over the railroad tracks and the fresh vegetable packing shed where half the town worked. Then they were almost to the beach. They passed the State Park trailer camp and the private trailer camps that huddled around it like vultures. Breakfast time for the birds. Beyond the reserve lay the hot dog stands, clam chowder stands, clam fork rental stands, the cycle rental shop where Pat worked, and the beach cabins for rent where Mr. Varian, his grand-daughter Mary, and the car were waiting.

"Why don't I know Mr. Varian?" Dad was asking. Nosey as usual. All teachers had this tendency to mind other people's business, and Dad was no exception.

Try going to a high school where your Dad was a teacher. Privacy? Ha.

"Probably because he just got here a couple of months ago from Las Vegas. He's a prospector. Says it pays about the same as Welfare but saves filling out all the forms. Of course, now that his granddaughter lives with him, I'll bet his wings will be clipped for a year or so. Right now, there's kind of a power struggle going on over who's going to rule the roost." Pat laughed.

"Well, I don't blame her for not wanting him to sell the car," Mike found himself saying.

His father looked at him briefly in the rear view mirror before continuing his conversation with Pat. "You mean he lives by prospecting for gold? Remarkable in this day and age. And I certainly envy him his freedom from forms. How did you find out about the car?"

"Gold, too, but semiprecious stones are his specialty. He found almost a mountainside of flowering obsidian. My psych teacher would say he's the frontier type, I guess."

"And how would your psych teacher type you?" Dad asked as they turned into a gravel driveway. A seabeaten sign almost covered in purple bougainvillea advertised cabins by the week or the month. They drove to a back cabin set slightly apart from the rest. Only a stand of wind stripped yellow lupine separated the peeling white cabin from the thirty foot sand dunes. The dunes overshadowed and menaced the little circle of houses, as if they had them ambushed. Several enormous pieces of driftwood and three glass floats stood in front of the Varian porch. Instead of a garden, Mike decided. Two battered purple velvet sofas flanked the steps below the covered porch. Mr. Varian put down his newspaper and climbed up from the broken springs in one of the sofas. He stood a moment, stretched, shook his head as if to clear it, and came to meet them.

"Nice of you to come by. My, you certainly do favor your boy, Mike, in looks, Mr. Lamon. Quite a resemblance," Mr. Varian said, shaking hands all around.

Both Mike and his father blushed. Mike always had the uncomfortable feeling that his father might be a preview of himself in another quarter century whenever people said this, which they did about once a month. Actually if he didn't also inherit his dad's disposition, it could be worse. Dad stood tall and straight and without any sign of a paunch, and he still had his hair, though gray wasn't much improvement over the no-color-straw of Mike's own hair.

"Yes, I feel as if I'm twenty years past my prime every time I look at him," Mike's father said. He turned and looked between the dunes toward the beach instead. "It's been a long while since I've been down to the beach before the tourists. I'd forgotten how many birds we have. I used to come clamming

Sunday mornings, but I've stuck home with the Sunday paper these last few years. Have you come to live here, Mr. Varian?"

"I guess the pelicans and the ducks are just passing through, migrating," Mr. Varian said hesitantly. "Yes, I'd like to make my home here——about half time."

Mike waited to see if his father would ask what the old prospector intended to do the other half. Prospecting, most likely, but he hoped his father wouldn't pry. Pat pointed toward what must be the dune buggy, covered with an old tarpaulin.

"Let's go," Mike whispered, but the two men continued looking out toward the ocean. Pat shrugged. He means don't rock the boat, Mike thought.

"Well, I'll be honest with you, Mr. Varian," Mr. Lamon said, finally. "I don't like the idea of Mike's buying a car before he has his license, but the money's his own and it's burning a hole in his pocket. If there were bus service around here, I'd say no car until he's eighteen, but there isn't bus service and so we're stuck. I have an uneasy feeling about Mike driving, but it's probably only my own wild youth nagging. So, if he's willing to put the car in my name, leave the key with Pat, and only drive with him or myself we might give it a try. I just wanted to let you know it's conditional before we take up your time, sir."

"Well, Mike?" Mr. Varian asked.

Mike nodded. How the hell could he know before he saw the car? Why didn't that old man take that canvas off? But they seemed to be waiting for him to say something, something positive.

"I'll cut football workout tomorrow and get the driving permit if you can go with me, Dad?"

"Fair enough. But don't go backing me into a corner about this, Mike. O.K.? We're just going for a trial run this morning. Then I'll take a look under the hood. Pat's a better judge than I am, though, and he says you take mighty good care of your engine, Mr. Varian."

Mike nodded. Who was backing who into a corner? Maybe Pat was shoving them both. Well! At last the old man was going over to unveil the car.

Mr. Varian smiled. "Well, I guess the proof is in the pudding," he said and whipped the tarp off the buggy as if he were unveiling one of the seven wonders of the world.

Mike stared. The car stood in a spotlight of morning sun like a little green frog ready to leap. He'd forgotten how little it was. Dusty, too. He'd have to give it a wax job. Couldn't be more than four or five years old. The paint and the black leather upholstery looked perfect. Like new. Mr. Varian was pumping air into the oversize airplane tires so they'd be firm enough for the highway. He'd have to remember that. He ought to check it over or at least pretend he was or they'd think he was seven kinds of idiot. But he just couldn't stop staring. That little green popcorn machine, it was going to be his. Probably not. Oh, yes, it was! He was going to climb in that little turtle on wheels and go hopping over the dunes like a rabbit —spilling a wake of sand, maybe drag racing, maybe chasing the surf. He was going to be a dune rider like there'd never been, and no father on earth was going to stop him! Motorcycles? Just hopped up bikes was all. *This* was a car.

"Hey, look who's just seen Christmas morning," Pat said grinning at him. "Let's take off."

"Thanks, Pat," Mike replied quietly.

"Neat little half pint at that," Mr. Lamon said, easing his long body into the small back seat.

Pat drove as if he'd handled a buggy all his life. Mr. Varian showed him the gears just once because he was used to an automatic transmission. Pretty good driving, and Mike was grateful. All he'd have to do with Dad jammed in back was to throw them around a little and that would be the end of one ride and one green car. Mike watched his father closely for the familiar sarcastic smirk but could detect nothing but a mild listening look. He was just listening. For what? Transmission whine? Clutch clatter?

A train whistle cut through the morning breeze, shrill and startling. Was that Paul's train? Was it stopping at a dozen towns along the coast this morning and picking up its draft quota on its way to Fort Ord? Would Pat rather be at the station seeing Paul off? But he'd said that Paul only wanted his family at the station. Impossible to tell from the back of his head what Pat was thinking. Paul was Pat's best friend. Maybe he wanted to be very busy this morning so he wouldn't have to think about Paul taking off for Fort Ord and points west? One of Pat's pet theories was that you didn't brood about things you couldn't change. The only way to avoid the draft was to stay in school, and Paul either couldn't or didn't want to. How did Paul feel this morning? What did he think as he hoisted his duffle bag aboard the train and looked back on the empty Sunday morning streets for what might be the last time?

"Is this the car you really want?" Dad asked quietly so that they wouldn't hear in the front seat.

"What?" Mike asked. "Did you ask me something?"

His father looked at him. "You're mighty quiet all of a sudden. I wondered if you've given up the motorcycle in favor of the buggy."

Mike shrugged, and the moment he did he knew it was a mistake. His father immediately had his I-never-do-anything-right-no-matter-how-hard-I-try look. Could he explain that he'd been thinking of something else, something more important than the car? Hardly. Not this morning. Actually he'd forgotten all about the motorcycle the moment the tarp was yanked off and he saw *this* car in the early morning sunlight. No Honda, even the 450, could begin to compare. Damn, damn, damn, the car had been as good as his, and he'd probably queered the whole deal with what Mom called his insolent shrug. What would wipe the mourning look from his father's face? Could he say that he'd been thinking about Paul? Pat might hear. Finally he said—

"I'd forgotten all about the motorcycle."

His father looked startled but did not answer.

They were heading up the thirty-five degree road to the mesa now, and the buggy drove as effortlessly as if they were still on the flat. Soon they'd leave the road and head for the open mesa country where they could try her out without roads. Then, if she did well, Pat would head for the dunes. That was the acid test. How would she do on the dunes? But now there was the other question too. Would Dad let the test go on or explode because Mike had shrugged and been an insolent kid once again?

He hadn't even meant the shrug. If only he could say something to erase the shrug, to strike it from the record. Not much chance. After all, who could believe that he'd forgotten all about a motorcycle after two years of progress reports on the motorcycle fund, a room papered with cycle pinups, and monthly feasibility battles. It was pretty hard to believe even when it happened to you. It just happened. Mr. Varian ripped the tarpaulin off this little green sand hopper and that was it. But why should Dad believe such a crazy story?

Of course, he *could* talk about carburetors or transmissions, but that would only remind Dad that he knew nothing about them and had promised to learn before he even mentioned the subject of cars again.

Probably best to just shut up while he was ahead. At least Dad hadn't roared out to turn the damn car around, that they were going home.

"Must be a couple dozen of them and honkers at that," Mr. Varian said.

"The old game warden must be having a stroke. Five hundred dollar fine on honker geese, but there's still always some fool who likes to play the long odds," Pat added.

"What?" Mike asked, thinking this was the first time Pat had spoken since he started to drive. Must be a silence record for him. Maybe he was thinking about Paul. Why were they stopping? Oh. Pat had pulled over to the side so they could watch the geese. They came through every fall, and yet Mike could never get used to watching such great proud enormous white geese go into a frenzy when they broke formation. Like someone had lost the football and the whole team was going nuts hunting for it before the other side took possession. No wonder he used to dream about those old honker geese.

"Five hundred dollars apiece?" Mr. Varian asked. "That's a lot of money. I knew a man once who shot a honker. I don't suppose he could have made it through the winter without that meat. He put up what he couldn't eat right off and it lasted over a month. That's how much meat that goose had. Of course, that was thirty years ago and more and there weren't any restrictions—or they weren't known. My friend was a young man then and strong as your boys, Mr. Lamon, though *his* muscles came from prospecting and living off the land. I went out with him two years, but this particular story takes place before I met up with him. All right, I *will* tell you the story.

"As I say, he was powerfully built. Winter was closing in fast in the high Sierra and he could expect snow most any day. He had to choose between trying to make it out without snowshoes or staying the winter, which meant being snowed in three months. He'd always wanted to go through a Sierra winter and there was another reason he wanted to stay this particular time. That was a gold claim he'd found, which might amount to nothing but might be a bonanza. Anyhow, he'd never have any peace until he knew.

"But there was no use pretending he had the food. He'd laid in a supply of staples but counted on catching his fresh meat and Lord only knew how he'd tried. He'd shot at every migrating flock of ducks and geese until his trigger finger first got raw and finally callused. He was so discouraged he almost didn't drag himself out to bother with this one. Matter of fact he shot from the porch and thought he'd missed until the most mournful cry hit the mountain stillness. You could just feel it splitting the earth itself with its sadness. Then there was a moan like an earthquake and an answering moan, from the mate, I imagine. So my friend figured he'd wounded the bird and in common decency he'd better go out and track him down and finish the job, though the bird's cry had dampened his enthusiasm for dinner.

"Well, sir, he searched all that morning and about decided the bird had either flown on or had landed so high in one of those jack pines he'd never be able to reach the creature if he *could* see it. At any rate, there were no more human moans. Finally, in the early afternoon, on his way home by another route, he found the bird. It wasn't dead yet, but the bullet had gone clean through the neck, through the black stripe they call a mourner's ribbon. He just looked at my friend with those black beady eyes and tried to move his great wings. He seemed so alive and bewildered. The man had to close his eyes or he could never have pulled the trigger, though he knew the bird's neck was broken. The goose died in an instant, and I think it was glad to go.

"So there was a down payment on food for the winter if he could only get it back to the cabin. The bird must have measured nearly ten feet from wing tip to wing tip and weighed twenty-five pounds or more. You can't know when you admire them in the sky what monsters they are to haul over rocks and fallen trees and how they cling to the frozen earth. He had to grab hold of the head and pull sharp before rigor mortis set in and his troubles were doubled. He hauled the bird home, sick in heart and stomach, and it was well after dark before they gained the porch of the cabin. He could get the stiffened goose no farther, and to leave it on the porch all night was inviting all the carnivores in the neighborhood to feast.

"So he built a huge fire and set himself to guard. At first he kept busy gathering wood. But he was so exhausted he feared falling asleep on his feet and then the morning would show little trace of him or the honker. The only thing to do was to start plucking the bird then and there to keep himself awake. He singed and plucked all that night; and the next day he cut up the bird and roasted some and boiled some until just the smell of goose was enough to sicken him the rest of his life. What he couldn't eat, he canned in every stray crock or jar and sealed with candle wax. He was just cleaning up when the snow began to fall. It fell for the three days and nights while he slept. By the time he woke, he was snowed in. He ate the honker and was grateful to the bird for making it possible to stay on near his claim, but once that winter was over he never ate fowl again. He never spent another winter in the high Sierra for that matter."

"And was it a rich claim?" Pat asked.

"Not a blamed thing there worth bothering about as it turned out. You might say it was a hard lesson in leaving flying geese be," Peter Varian finished wryly.

The geese were circling back into formation, and the four men in the car watched them silently until they were only dark specks in the blue sky.

"What was your friend's name?" Mike said finally.

"You know, it was all so long ago I've even forgotten that—what a garrulous old fool I'm becoming," the prospector said, shaking his head.

That was a damn fool thing to ask. Any fool could see he was probably telling his own story. It must be terrible to watch something die. The only time he ever saw an animal die was when a sea lion washed up on the beach and flopped his head once and stopped breathing. That was all. Five years ago.

That same summer he'd found a silver dollar in an old pair of pants washed up in another tide. If he got this car, he could really go beachcombing after a storm. He could cover the whole ten mile stretch in a day and get the pick of everything washed up in a storm tide before the tourists got to it.

"Let's go. Please," Mike said aloud. They were parked near the edge of the mesa so that the town and the dunes and the ocean fanned out below. The dirt road they were going to take down dropped straight off the mesa to the sand dunes below. Dune riders came from all over the state to take "Devil's Slide"; and the road had gotten guttier and guttier. If the little hopper could take a road like that without turning over and dumping them, it could take anything. Talk about an acid test.

"Are you ready?" Pat asked.

"Let her roll!" Mr. Varian yelled, excited.

"As ready as I'll ever be," Mr. Lamon groaned.

Pat nodded to his father and grinned. Without another word he gunned the engine and swung the buggy to the right and onto "Devil's Slide." They hung an instant on the lip of the mesa and then plunged over the edge onto the rutted, rocky, dusty cattle trail that joined the high land with the dunes. He drove at a breakneck pace, almost as if he were daring the buggy to flip and send them rolling. Mike kept expecting his father to reach forward and turn the key in the ignition, but he didn't. He didn't even tell Pat to slow down. Of course, the wilder Pat drove, the more chance there was of something going wrong. Dad was sure listening. It was hard to tell when they kept hitting rocks, but there did seem to be a knock. That meant transmission trouble, didn't it?

"Let's take her over the dunes to the gun club and then back along the beach to your house, Mr. Varian. That is, if you don't mind, sir?" Dad suggested.

"Grand with me. Wonderful short cut you found, Pat."

"Reminds me of a roller coaster! Just lucky your granddaughter isn't here. She wouldn't like us treating her buggy this way." Mike tried to laugh lightly. He'd wondered all morning why Mary hadn't come with them.

"Who, Mary? Don't worry about Mary. Her bark's worse than her bite. Fine girl if I do say so. I hope to take her prospecting with me next summer, as a matter of fact. That's why I'd like to wean her to a motorcycle."

"Prospecting? Well, if any girl could take to prospecting it would be her. Mike thought she might be waiting for us with a shotgun this morning." Pat laughed.

"She would have been if she'd thought of it. She's sitting home hoping we'll run out of gas or get stuck, I imagine. But she'll get over it. You'll like Mary when you get to know her, Mike. She doesn't hold grudges."

"Maybe he already likes her," Pat teased.

Mike blushed. If he said anything nice, Pat would never get off his back. Fortunately they hit a gully and had all they could do to hang on. The gully seemed to be the dividing line between cattle path and sand dunes because after lurching wildly for about fifty feet they started to climb into loose sand. The engine churned a little, struggling. Pat shifted into low, and it seemed to grab hold. Was that the way it was supposed to act? Mike hoped so. He felt the sharp sting of sand in his eyes. Without a roof or windows, the dune came right at you. He blinked against the glare of the sand. The wheels spun and then dug into the shifting grainy dune, and Pat took them straight up, straight up twenty feet, straining the car so it seemed as if it just had to stop the very next foot all the way up and did not and kept going until finally they swung over the lip and ran smoothly along the crest. It was like coming out of a cocoon of whirling sand into the sun again. Mike felt he'd be choking sand for a week.

"Takes a good engine to pull that," Dad said approvingly.

"Now watch this," Pat said, and he spun the car along the top edge of the dune bowl so that they hung cockeyed from the crest, two wheels hugging the top and two running along inside the inverted bowl. Flying must be like that, at least flying in an old open cockpit plane. This was the outer limits, the stretch. The wheels spun again as they hit the bottom of the dune and the car scooped sand.

"Careful. Keep going. Keep going," Mr. Varian warned.

Pat shifted into low and dug deeper into the sand. The wheels spun a shower of sand over them.

"Damn."

"Easy, Pat. Don't stop. Keep gunning it," Dad shouted.

"Just keep at it, Pat. She'll do it."

"Rock it, son. Rock it."

The car lifted and spun. Maybe. Maybe. No, she was down in, digging in. Deeper. All they needed was to get stuck. God. Don't let us get stuck, Mike thought. Keep grinding, grinding. Silence. Pat had turned off the ignition.

"That's it. I'm afraid we've had it," Pat said.

"But we're five miles from anywhere," Mike groaned, looking at his father. He looked grim.

MARY'S REVENGE

THEY SAT in the buggy waiting for the shower of sand to subside so they could see how badly they were stuck. Mike had sand in his hair, shoes, down his shirt and even between his teeth. That meant Dad did too. And that meant trouble.

"I don't suppose we have any boards?" Dad asked, opening the door and stretching as he unfolded himself out of the car.

"Wouldn't likely need them if we did, which we do not," Mr. Varian answered and then added, "Sure is a fine day. Just look at that lizard go, will you?"

A startled lizard scurried out from under the car and streaked across the dune, losing itself finally under a sage bush. Mr. V. was right. It *was* a fine day if all you had to worry about was the sun. They were stuck in one of those dune coves that formed an oasis. A stand of willow trees grew along one side of the hollow and yellow flowers bloomed from the edges of the trees. If you dug down half a dozen feet, you'd probably hit fresh water.

There was a fresh tang of salt and sage to the air. It was like another world; and Mike thought that if only Dad weren't along with his life and death power of attorney, it wouldn't be such a bad spot to be stuck. Of course, they *were* a good five miles from town.

Mike looked at Pat who was sadly shaking his head. "I mean those wheels dug in. Sorry Dad. Guess I should have gunned her harder and faster."

"Faster yes, but gun her any harder and you'd have flipped us all. No, you did all right, Pat. Just the breaks of the game. Maybe, if you and Mike go on out to the beach, you can find enough driftwood boards to lay under the wheels and help us out."

Mr. Varian was grinning from ear to ear. "Sir," he said, "no need to make a mountain out of a molehill. Two of us can take the front and two the back and we can just lift that half-pint buggy up and right angle her away from the hill and if I'm not misled by past experience, she'll take right off. This is just a little old bug, no bigger than a sand flea."

"You're kidding?" Mike asked tentatively.

"No, sir, I'm not."

"Well, here goes nothing, jack rabbit," Pat said, hoisting one fender.

"Hold on, Pat. Let's dig out around the wheels first. Why lift farther than you have to?" Mr. Varian suggested.

"This little buggy of yours dug in like a sand crab," Dad said as they pawed the sand away from the wheels with their hands.

"Of mine?" Mike asked, holding his breath. "Of mine?"

"Is this what you want? Six hundred is a good price, but from your point of view it's a lot of money. And you'll have to get a Saturday job to maintain it."

"Oh, yes! Thanks, Dad, thanks."

"Don't thank me. I'm not the one who's paying for it. And remember the conditions, Mike."

Mike nodded. The buggy was his. In spite of getting stuck, in spite of everything, he now owned a turtle on wheels. He looked at the sleek green fiber glass body and shook his head. It was too much, just too much! He had never even dared to think he might have a car like this, and then there it was. Perfect. Thanks to Pat.

"Pat! Pat!"

"Don't panic. I'll help you. We're almost free up here."

"No, I mean she's mine. Dad says I can have her!

Really!"

"Hallelujah!" Pat shouted. And then he was pumping Mike's hand.

"Hey, take it easy. I haven't won the Grand Prix, after all—yet!"

"And it's up to you to teach him to drive, Pat. Safely!"

"And tomorrow we get the permit?" Mike asked.

His father nodded. "Providing, of course, that Mr. Varian is still willing to sell?"

They all turned to the old prospector who stood watching them, a little apart. He ran his hand over the sleek hood. "Well, old grasshopper, it looks like you've got a new owner. See that you behave yourself!" He winked at Mike. "She's yours if we lift her out of here!"

"O.K. Grasshopper, get ready to leap," Pat said.

"Let's see you put those football muscles to good use for a change, Mike," Dad added.

Mike was surprised at how light the buggy was. They were able to pick her up and angle her enough to start the first time. The worst part was sinking into the sand themselves. Mr. Varian let a little more air out of the tires. They cut between the dunes when they started again. Pat took no more chances.

Mike hardly remembered the ride home. He was worried that his mother would say no, that the old prospector's granddaughter might say no and make it stick, that Dad would have a change of heart, that Mr. Varian wouldn't be able to part with his "grasshopper," that the bank had burned down and his money was gone.

By the next afternoon none of these calamities had struck and Mike stood outside the door of the Motor Vehicle Department with his father. It was a gray day, a perfect day for flunking an exam, and Mike pushed the door open reluctantly.

The room was bare and sparsely furnished and looked like a gray maze. The partitions separating petitioners from employees looked like mazes in the rat cages in biology class. Long lines of applicants stood in front of every window waiting to take their written test or their eye test or pay fines or get permission slips. They hunched, bit their nails, smoked and then ground their cigarettes into the floor vehemently and, though you couldn't catch anyone laughing, a self-conscious giggle hung over the room. You could smell fear, too, in the perspiration, the heavy perfume, and stale cigarette smoke. About a dozen people stood at a narrow elbow-high ledge running along one end of the room working on awkward sheets of paper about two feet long. That must be the permit test. They didn't look as if it was any lead pipe cinch! Pat said he had it cold, but maybe they'd all thought so too before they came.

About half the applicants were kids from school, and they looked strange in good clothes. No one he knew well. The girls wore heels and stockings. A driving test must be murder in heels, if you weren't

44

used to them. However, the Driver Education teachers said examiners were rough on anyone who looked sloppy, and there was no percentage in fighting with the examiner. A license meant wheels and freedom.

Mike sighed. He would have been quite willing to postpone the test, except for Dad and Mr. Varian. They'd arranged to pay for the car and collect the pink slip from Peter Varian after the test. "To celebrate," Mr. Varian had said. This could be one very sour celebration if he didn't pass! He might even lose the car because the old prospector couldn't wait forever.

"Did you bring your driver education slip with your age and grade?" Dad asked, and Mike nodded. Did his *A* in the course count for anything? What line was he supposed to join?

Dad chose window 14. The wall clock said three-forty. What time did they close? Would they make it? How long did he get for the test? Mike felt in his pocket. He'd brought both a pen and a pencil because he didn't know which they required on the test. It would be easier to use the pencil and erase. Glasses? Where were they? Could he possibly have been so stupid that he forgot his glasses? He tried his jacket and shirt pockets. No luck. His father was looking at him curiously.

"Dad, I forgot my glasses. They're in my gym locker."

"Good Lord, do you need them? Too late to go

45

back. We've got less than an hour as it is. Actually —it's a good idea to pass the eye test without glasses if you can, not that you'd usually drive without them, of course, but just in case."

At least he wasn't mad. There wasn't going to be a lecture on wasting other people's time or organization being next to Godliness, or lack of responsibility. Thank God. He *had* taken one eye test in school without the glasses and passed, but this was bound to be a lot stiffer. He didn't use them half the time but —face it—he'd muffed this time but good. Maybe they'd let him take the written test and have Dad sign for it and he could come back tomorrow for the eye exam. But even then they still couldn't buy the buggy today, and Mr. Varian wasn't going to hang on forever. Not when he had an urge for a motorcycle like he did. He just wasn't the waiting type! Mike thought about the wild soaring ride over the dunes and down the beach yesterday. He could have made that run every day of his life and he was about to lose it all because he forgot to bring his glasses—just one little oversight.

"You're next, Mike. Better get out the documents."

O.K. He could *see* he was next. He could at least see that. And come to think of it, that consolation line of Dad's about doing without the glasses wasn't so happy either. Dad only kept his temper when things were really serious.

"These seem to be in order," the woman said in a

tone that implied they probably weren't but she hadn't the time or inclination to challenge him at the moment and so in charity she'd let it pass. She handed back the test and told him to mark it in pencil. Nothing about a time limit. She turned her attention to Dad, who stood behind Mike.

"Oh, no, thanks just the same. I'm not in line. Just here to sign the permit for my son. Sure wish you had coffee for nervous fathers, though," he told the clerk.

"Then would you mind stepping out of the line? Next!"

Coffee! God, what a dumb remark. He was taking a test, not being born. Oh, well. Mike scanned the test for hidden traps. The questions seemed straight. They were all true-false or multiple choice. He checked them off in a few minutes, hesitating over speed in passing a school bus and maximum speed for a car pulling a trailer. He wasn't going to be pulling any trailer with his beach buggy, so he hadn't paid much attention to that section in the Motor Vehicle Code. Finished.

Was that all? He glanced at the two girls next to him, both good-looking and both bewildered. A middle-aged man on the other side of him was chewing the end of his pencil. He marked, erased, changed an answer again. Better read it over again. Maybe they hadn't studied. All of them? *He* must have goofed. Better change the answer to the maximum trailer speed. Maybe the right turn question was wrong. Better not worry it. Dad said first instinct was usually right in true-false and multiple choice. After all, you *could* miss six and still pass.

Nevertheless, Mike watched worriedly while the man behind the window labeled PERMIT looked over his paper. He scribbled 100% across the top of the sheet. Well. How about that!

"Good work, son. Now let's check your vision. Try the fifth line down on the chart directly in front of you."

The man pointed to a chart halfway across the room. The top central *E* was clear enough, but five lines down the letters had rings like those around the moon before a rain. Well, either try to read them or bolt for the door. It was too late to admit needing glasses now and much too late to run over to the five and ten cent store and buy some. Here goes nothing, Mike thought, and went through the letters quickly, hoping an error here and there might be lost in the shuffle. It was impossible to tell from the examiner's bored face whether he'd made it or not. He covered each eye in turn with a white index card and went through the whole process again. The letters were clearer with one eye than with two. That had been true with the eye test at school too. The inspector wrote hieroglyphics on a form. Just tell me how I'm doing, Mike willed. Please tell me how I'm doing. The examiner said nothing. He was still bored, and that might be a good sign. After all, it must be a little more exciting when someone flunks. The examiner pulled over a two foot square black box equipped with what looked like stereoptican lenses and adjusted it to Mike's face.

"Now just relax. This tests your depth perception and doesn't hurt a bit. Where do you see the square with the dots? Up, down, right, or left. All rightee, now. And now. And now. Again. And now. That's all. Have your mother and father sign this slip and bring it back to us."

"My father's here now," Mike said weakly, still not sure whether he'd passed or not. Dimly he heard the inspector say he'd passed one hundred percent on the written work and, though his vision wasn't perfect, it probably was a nervous reaction since he saw better with one eye than with both.

Dad signed the permit slip with a flourish. "Mike always does well on written work," he said. "I just hope he doesn't figure he knows it all after this."

"Sometimes turns out that way, but your boy seems a sensible kid," the man said kindly.

"Did you just *have* to say that?" Mike exploded on their way to the car. Did Dad *have* to spoil everything every *single* time he accomplished anything?

"Say what? Oh, that about the written work? For heaven's sake, Mike, can't you even take a joke? Now look, if you're going into one of your sulks, I'll just go on home and correct my history exams and we'll see Mr. Varian another time. I don't have to do this,

49

you know. Make up your mind now."

Dad had what Pat called the hands on the hips ultimatum look. Mike stood facing him, his fists clenched. If he could only just walk off, just once when Dad pulled this stunt. But he only did it when the odds were high and that was what was so unfair. He knew perfectly well that if they didn't buy the car now, it would probably be gone. To say nothing of how they looked standing here having a staredown in the middle of the parking lot.

"Let's go," Mike said softly.

"Would you like to drive over to Peter Varian's?" Dad asked, holding the door by the driver's side open.

Peace offering, Mike thought. He must know Pat had been giving him driving lessons on the side. Pat should know enough to keep his mouth shut. Talking always got somebody in trouble. He'd always wanted to drive the Oldsmobile, but not today, not when he felt so kooky he'd run smack into the first available telephone pole. But Dad was being generous, and if he were rejected, it would be a sure symptom of sulking, proof positive. He didn't have much choice. Mike started to slide in behind the wheel and then he remembered.

"Maybe I'd better wait for the glasses," he said.

"Lord, yes. Stupid of me to forget. I wondered if my glasses might have helped you—probably not. But it is better to wear the glasses, sometimes helps to stop in time."

Dad was disappointed, but they were both in the clear. Mike began to breathe easier. At least he *had* passed. Whatever else, he had passed. They drove by the high school, and he could see the football team just trotting in from the practice field to the showers. This was the first practice he'd missed and probably had better be the last or there'd be a new varsity fullback. Lots of more experienced guys around. But he wouldn't miss any more, and tomorrow he could tell them about the perfect score. Or wait until someone asked and then just mention it, offhand. Wouldn't seem quite such a brag that way. Forgetting the glasses would make a good tale too. Of course, most of the team already had licenses and they could go on for hours about wild rides and wilder dates. But at least he wouldn't be quite so out of it, quite such a kid, especially with a status buggy like the Grasshopper.

"Looks like Mr. Varian's had a new wax job done for you. Decent of him," Dad said as they pulled up the driveway under the purple bougainvillea vine and drew alongside the dune buggy.

"Hey, that's bitchin', man." Mike meant both the wax job and the sleek green convertible buggy itself. There was something whole, of a piece about the way this car looked. Like an expensive sport car. That was probably the molded fiber glass shell. Only the tires, the twist of exhaust piping, and the exposed rear engine mushroomed from beneath the smooth body. It might have Volkswagen components, but it had more class than the bug, a lot more class.

"Congratulations," Mr. Varian said, pulling Mike up on the porch and into the house. "Driving's one of the great pleasures of my life, and I hope it will be for you. That's why I wanted you to have my hopper. She's a good buggy, and she deserves to be somebody's first. And that's the truth, Mary."

"Yes, Grandpa."

"How did you know I passed?" Mike asked and didn't hear the answer. He was staring at Mary. Did she know he'd been going out of his way to avoid her at school because he felt so grim about taking her car? Not that she'd care *how* he felt unless it was bad enough to drop dead! She was sitting at the kitchen table peeling apples, which meant that she didn't even have to look at him. She was wearing a bright red pants suit that did a lot for her. She was beautiful all right. And about as friendly as the most distant star in the sky. Well, if it was going to be a choice between the girl and the car, then the car won.

"Let's just get the preliminaries over, and we can all go for a spin in Mike's jalopy," Mr. Varian said.

"Do you think it's going to ride different because he owns it?" Mary asked haughtily.

"I just might take everyone by the showroom where my new Honda 450 is waiting for me to spring it," he continued.

"You *promised* I could have first ride! And learn to drive it. You promised!" Mary accused, jumping up.

Then she sat down and went on peeling apples.

"First time I've ever seen Mary so interested in her work," Mr. Varian teased as he left the room.

Mary flushed, and when she looked up Mike saw tears in her eyes. It was mean to tease her like that. Mike hoped her grandfather'd at least keep his promise to let her drive the motorcycle. And she could drive the buggy, too, if she wanted. Lord, better watch it. What was he getting into? Nothing, because Mary wouldn't touch him with a ten foot pole! And probably just as well. He'd already had one date, and on that occasion the girl had spent the entire evening edging away from him as if he wanted to rape her. Her attitude hadn't made for relaxed conversation, and Mike hadn't been in any hurry to try another date since.

Mr. Varian and Mr. Lamon were rummaging in the bedroom, looking for guarantees, the pink slip, all the paper pertaining to the dune buggy. Mike looked over at Mary, and her green eyes sparkled. She was actually laughing—at him or herself? At any rate her whole face lit up, as if she were an electric light and someone had switched her on.

But she didn't say anything, and Mike didn't know what to say so he looked around the room, casually, he hoped. The cabin might have been built of driftwood. The floor was bare, and the furniture was very simple. There were two more comfortable old velvet sofas, red this time, and a couple of willow garden chairs with big cushions propped in them. A kitchen table, four chairs, a small bookcase, and an expensive shortwave portable radio-phonograph completed the furniture. A narrow ledge ran around the room at eye level, and dozens of model railroad engines sat jauntily along it. Where did Mr. Varian get those? And why weren't there any rocks or gold nuggets from his prospecting? It was more like a cabin on a ship than a house.

"Granddaddy carved the model trains," Mary said unexpectedly. "He says they're like keeping a diary. He only has to look at them, remember when and where he made each one, and it brings back every prospecting trip he's made since he and grandma started out thirty years ago. He usually keeps them in an old sea trunk, and when I was a little girl I'd just go and pick one out and he'd tell me the story."

"Man, that must have been great. Mary, I want to tell you something before your grandfather and Dad come back. When you get your license, I just want you to know you're welcome to borrow the buggy anytime you want."

"Please, Mike, it's going to be all right. Just don't —be nice to me," Mary said, looking as if she were going to cry again. She got up and stood with her nose pressed to the window, looking out. "It's going to storm. You can tell by the butterflies."

"What butterflies?" Mike didn't see any butterflies. Mary was right about the storm, though. The

54

sky, which had been gray, was black and the ocean ominously still. There wasn't a bird in sight, which meant that the beach had battened itself down for the first storm of the year.

Mary pointed to the lone eucalyptus tree standing between them and the dunes. It was bent almost double to the will of the wind. Gradually Mike realized that there was something strange, something different about this tree from other trees in a storm. It was quivering, quivering because the tree was completely covered with butterflies! They were camouflaged because they were perched so that the underside of the brown and orange and white wings, the muted tones, were exposed. Protective coloring. But how it helped against the indiscriminate fury of a storm was difficult to explain. In a crisis you must do the only thing you've ever found to save yourself, Mike decided.

"They're monarchs, and they're on their way to Mexico for the winter. I've been watching them for two weeks now, but with the cold and rain I guess they'll move on," Mary said sadly. "Not that *you* care."

"How do you know what I care—oh, you mean, because I'm nothing but a dumb athlete," Mike said bitterly. "I'll bet I know this beach and the dunes better than you ever will—"

"You didn't know about the butterflies," Mary reminded him. "Actually, though, I didn't mean anything except—"

55

"Except what?"

Just then Mr. Varian and Mike's Dad returned to the kitchen and dumped armloads of papers on the kitchen table.

"Hey, watch out for my apples," Mary yelled.

"Your father here tells me you passed at the top of the class, one hundred percent today. Can't do better than that," Mr. Varian said.

Mike felt himself blushing. So Dad thought it was at least worth mentioning. Even Mary looked impressed. "Just dumb luck," he said.

"Nonsense. Well done. Shall we see if the buggy still runs now that she's yours? Where *did* I put those keys? I could have sworn I left them right here on top of the mantel. Saw them just an hour or so ago. I know I did. Get absentminded when you grow old. Where *are* they?"

"We really ought to be getting back pretty soon or Mike's mother will think we flunked or got lost or Lord knows what. She's a worrier," Dad said as he began to look for the keys, too.

Mike knew even before he looked at Mary's grin. If he didn't have the keys, he couldn't take possession. It was as simple as that. Hiding the keys wouldn't do her any permanent good, but it made a slick protest. And the other set of keys was probably missing, too.

"Darn it, I had another set of keys, but I lost them just last week. The first day you came, in fact. Meant to have some more made. Just forgot, as usual. Must be here, somewhere," Mr. Varian said predictably, searching through the pockets of his jackets.

Mary stood looking out the window. The corners of her mouth kept twitching into a grin.

"Mary," he said.

"I guess we really should help them look, Mike." She was still watching the butterflies.

"Mary, give me the keys. You can keep one set. Just give me the others," Mike whispered.

Mary turned to him. "I don't know whatever on earth you're talking about," she said, batting her eyelashes.

"You look as if you're glad I found out, Scarlett O'Hara."

"Well, I'd hate to think everyone was that stupid —shhh, here it comes!"

"Mary! Mary, come here this instant! This isn't an Easter egg hunt, you know!" But the old man looked delighted, too. Anything for a joke. Crazy. It *was* pretty clever, after all. Besides, the out-of-it-all look on Dad's face was worth a thousand keys.

"No, you have to find them, both of you. It's only fair after selling the car out from under me. I won't be so mad at you either, Mike, if you have to work for your keys."

"I already worked for that damn car all last summer."

"Well, then, you've had experience. Good."

This time Dad smiled. His grin widened even more

when Mary said that under the rules of the key game *he* didn't have to look.

"I think I'd better call Mike's mother and tell her where we are and that we'll be bringing two guests home for dinner. All right?"

"Oh, we'd love to go to dinner, wouldn't we Granddaddy? Because then I won't have to cook. And I don't have any homework because tomorrow is Veterans' Day. We don't have to go to school tomorrow, Mike!"

"You'd kill *me* if I pulled a stunt like that," Mike growled at his father, who only raised one eyebrow and closed the door softly behind him. He honked the Grasshopper's horn as he passed.

"*That's* rubbing it in," Mike muttered as he cased the house, trying to decide where a girl like Mary might put two sets of keys.

"It's really obvious," Mary added helpfully.

"Be specific," Mike urged, on his way to the bedroom because it offered more hiding places and, therefore, probably had at least one set of keys. Mike looked through the drawers and tried to fold sweaters, pants and an astonishing variety of caps and put them back in the drawer neatly. They smelled of a sweet tobacco and of Ivory soap. Then he took the bed apart completely and, at Mr. Varian's suggestion, put clean sheets back on it. He even looked inside the toilet tank. No keys. He pulled out four boxes of papers and rock samples from under the bed because once Mary had hidden Mr. Varian's roll-your-own cigarette machine in those boxes to make him stop smoking. Mr. Varian picked up each railroad model and examined it carefully.

"You're just lucky I'm an indulgent old man, young lady," he said.

"Granddaddy, you haven't done your fall cleaning anyhow."

"Fall cleaning, my eye. I just moved in here."

The three of them stood looking at each other. It was an impasse, and it was getting late. Mom wouldn't like delaying dinner. Mike felt that if he called all-come-in-free that he'd never live it down. The very fact that her grandfather was not giving up showed that Mary was a poor winner. Besides, she wasn't going to beat him. On the other hand, this could go on forever. Mr. Varian started to say something and changed his mind. There was something stubborn about the way he sat down and something remarkably like Mary. No one spoke.

"Well, I never *said* they were in the house," Mary said finally.

"Now *that* is dirty pool," Mr. Varian said as he headed for the door.

Suddenly Mike knew why his father had honked the car horn. It would be just like Mary to leave the keys in the ignition, completely ignoring the fact that the car might be stolen. But maybe that was why she had spent so much time at the window. It was *such* an ideal place to leave the key and so damn simple. A real put down. Mike waited, longer than seemed necessary, until he heard the expected bellow from Mr. Varian.

"Would have served you right if Mr. Lamon had driven off and taught you a good lesson," he said as he came back holding both sets of keys above his head. "One was in the ignition and the other in the glove compartment," he added, glaring at Mary.

"He couldn't have left without me knowing because, if you will remember, Granddaddy, I stood here by the window the whole time."

"You *still* let us tear the house apart without saying one word about the fact that the yard was in bounds."

"Let's go see your old motorcycle and go on to dinner or we're going to be late. You can bawl me out later."

Mike was surprised that her grandfather agreed to readily but understood when he heard Mary groan as she opened the front door.

"All right, you win. *You win. Where'd* you put my bike?"

"Wouldn't you like to know?" asked her grandfather.

PROPHET OF THE
MARBLE ORCHARD

MIKE SAT in his dune buggy waiting impatiently for his father who had to be at least on his third cup of coffee. It must be nearly 10 A.M. Mike fiddled with the key in the ignition. Had it been only six weeks since the afternoon Mary had hidden the keys and made them search the house, when all the time they'd been right in the ignition? Only six weeks? It seemed more like a year. Six weeks ago he couldn't even drive. Not really. And now Pat said he could probably pass the test for the license if he had to. Six weeks ago he and Mary had hardly been speaking acquaintances, and tomorrow night he was taking her to the Lettermen's New Year's Eve Dance. Six weeks ago he had seen the Grasshopper for the first time, and now he could not imagine getting through a day without driving it. Six weeks ago they'd been in the middle of the football season, and now it was over. Too bad about that. Coming in third in the conference wasn't bad, but it wasn't a championship either.

Things had changed all right. All but one thing. He still had to wait for Dad to make a decision. Six weeks ago it was whether he could buy a car. Now it was whether he could drive Mary in that car six little blocks to the dance and back to her grandfather's house—by themselves and without Pat as an everlasting babysitter. This would mean bending the rules a little because he didn't have a license; but what, for God's sake, could happen along six blocks of back streets? Goodness knows he was a more careful driver than Pat, and his reaction time must be quicker than a man Dad's age. However, he intended to wait until after the ride they were about to take before he mentioned what he wanted to do.

If Dad didn't come, they were going to get caught in a storm. It was hovering, a probability of clouds and rising wind and freshness in the air. Maybe he should put the top up? Not yet. There was time, but not enough to waste drinking coffee that wasn't good for a man anyhow.

Dad was going to be surprised. Pat said he had the

instinct. Driving involved a lot more instinct than the driver training instructor, who was a real idiot, was willing to admit. That guy saw driving as one long struggle to reach a destination without killing someone, which was why kids called him the prophet of the marble orchard. He'd probably never exceeded a speed limit in his life. He'd sure never taken off down a beach in the early morning with the birds scattering in a thousand directions and the sea roaring along with the car and the wind and the sand in your face and your hair—not going anywhere to meet anyone but just soaring. Like Pat said, a car was better than a psychiatrist. Not that Mike was a speeder, but he could sure understand it. Which was more than could be said of that Driver Ed. teacher. You had to be too dumb to teach anything else in order to teach Driver Ed.

"Finally! I should think you'd want to see how I'm doing instead of spending all morning over a cup of caffeine nerves," Mike shouted to his father and mother who were standing at the front door talking.

"For your information, Mike, this is the coldest December in twenty-three years and, therefore, I am in no hurry to leave a warm house *and* your mother's company for a hair-raising ride in an open car."

"Yeah, I'll have to admit that Alaskan jacket you gave me is great for the beach this winter—but cold's good for you, starts the circulation. Hell, Mom, come on."

"One parent down with pneumonia is enough," Dad retorted.

"I'd like to, Mikey, really. But it's two days since Christmas and wrapping paper is still strewn over every inch of the house. You'll all be out from underfoot, so I can pick up."

"In other words, it's good riddance to bad rubbish," Dad quipped as he slid in next to Mike. Mike was annoyed that they were giving themselves brownie points for ignoring the "hell" he'd let slip so he wouldn't get nervous. Profanity usually brought one-day-restricted-to-the-house sentences, especially from Mom who was worried that people wouldn't admire her sons and, therefore her, if they used bad language.

"Pray that it doesn't rain before we get back." Dad shivered inside his poncho and pulled his navy cap down over his ears. He even had a wool scarf tightly wrapped around his neck. Mike had given everyone in his family a waterproof poncho and a navy surplus cap for Christmas so they could ride in the buggy comfortably and without acting as if they were making the world's ultimate sacrifice. Personally, he'd been wanting to drive through a storm. Mr. Varian told about driving through thunderstorms in the Sierras and said nature came right down and met you in a way she never could in a car that had a top to it.

"Hey, watch that clutch or you won't drive the *family* car, I can tell you that."

"Sorry. I don't usually grind the clutch." Mike

sighed. No alibis was a firm rule in the Lamon household. "Where to, the mesa or the dunes?"

"Let's try the highway to Berros. That's where your skill is going to count."

Mike looked at his father narrowly. The Berros freeway was the drag strip, and those were the same words the Driver Training Instructor had used. Followed by a tirade on what a competitive driver he was. Dad and the idiot taught in the same school. Oh, it was just great to attend a school where your father taught. Just great! If there'd been a casual conversation between those two buddies, this was going to be a long morning, a ten thousand hour morning. He and Mary would be walking to the dance for sure.

"You're the boss," Mike answered as casually as he could and was glad to see his father lean back and relax. He'd be gripping the roll bar for dear life if he'd talked to the prophet of the marble orchard.

So far, so good. Dad looked as if he was actually enjoying the drive. Now, the problem was to obey every rule so this whole thing would turn out all right. There was going to be rain. You could smell it in the air and the birds were going crazy. Birds seemed to feel they'd starve if they left one berry on one bush before a rain, even if they knew for sure it was just a shower. Even ducks whose wings were protected from water just went nuts before a rain.

They had the road almost to themselves for several miles. They'd cleared the town and were only twenty

65

miles or so from Berros when Mike saw a green Chevrolet coming towards them like a bat out of hell. It must have been doing ninety miles an hour and looked like it was straddling the white line. He swerved as it tore by them, and as he swerved he felt the asphalt give way to the dirt shoulder under the right wheels. Automatically he pulled back, was already back on the road when his father grabbed the wheel, swerving the buggy over the white line.

"Damn fool stunt. You could get us both killed." He let go of the wheel as suddenly as he'd grabbed it.

"But I had to pull over or we'd have been in a head-on crash. That character must have been doing ninety."

"He happens to have been completely on his side of the road, and he couldn't have been doing more than sixty. Anyone's car shy until he gets enough experience to judge distance. It all comes with time. Don't worry," Dad said calmly, deliberately.

Don't worry? Don't worry? Who grabbed the wheel and almost flipped them over? If he was mad, for God's sake why didn't he say so instead of adopting that patronizing when-you're-my-age-you'll-understand attitude? Talk about a middle-aged man being wound up like a Yo-Yo. He was a sure candidate for a heart attack.

"O.K., now turn left onto the freeway and let's see how you do with traffic alongside. It shouldn't be too bad on a Sunday morning. After all, we're early for the church crowd. Better stick to the right hand lane, though, and let what traffic there is fight for the other lanes." He pulled a blanket around himself against the rising wind.

"I've only driven on the freeway once before," Mike grumbled.

"Good. I told Pat to wait until I had the time to take you. The freeway *is* dangerous and too much responsibility for him to take. Good entrance, Mike. Now watch yourself as the traffic merges. Give the other fellow the right of way. You have to assume everyone else on the road is crazy. The rear mirror isn't enough—watch that side mirror!"

Just shut up and let me concentrate, Mike thought. There was only one white Plymouth near the entrance and four lanes in each direction. It would be hard to go wrong unless a backseat driver got you so flustered you couldn't see *anything*. Freeways were for the birds anyhow because it *was* true that you had to be all keyed up and worried about other drivers. But who needed a freeway? He just wanted the buggy for runs over the beach and the mesa and the dunes. He wanted the wild wind and the waves and the sting of salt on his cheeks.

Nobody understood this except Mary and her grandfather. Everyone thought he wanted to become a speed demon and drag a dozen kids through town at sixty miles an hour. Even Pat thought so. But if you've never had nor wanted a dozen wild friends, how was having a license going to change your basic nature? It wasn't. Dad was wasting his time trying to make the community safe from Mike Lamon. Live and let live. The only roads he was interested in were those to school and to Mary's grandfather's house. And his only interest in doing well on the freeway was to get Dad to let him drive the six blocks from Peter Varian's to the dance on New Year's Eve. Maybe he should make a clean breast of it, tell Dad the Mike Lamon thesis on driving and life? Why not? At least he could say he tried.

"Mike, for God's sakes, slow down! Where's the fire? Can't bear to have a single car pass, can you? You just have to speed up and race every car." Dad had suddenly hunched forward, was peering through the windshield tensely, chain smoking, and generally looking as if he were in the last lap of the Indianapolis.

"God, what did I do now? I was only keeping up with the traffic. I thought I was doing O.K." Mike forced his attention back to the road. Guiltily, he saw that the speedometer read five miles over the limit. No cop would give you a ticket for five miles. Still. He let up on the accelerator.

"No swearing. Look, Mike, it isn't just that you're going over the limit. You can't drive at the legal maximum all the time and certainly not in this wind with a light car like your Meyer Manx. Every driver has to gauge traffic, weather, and road conditions. But for an inexperienced driver like you, and six

68

weeks does not constitute much experience, forty-five should be your maximum under any circumstances. In fact, I'll make it a rule. Until I see that you *can* let other cars pass you are not to drive over forty-five miles an hour under any circumstances."

Mike said nothing. Here we go again, he thought. Dad was getting rid of excess adrenalin by making *another* rule. Later he often took them back. Mike sighed.

"Mike—"

"Dad, I'm trying! Lay off! Hell, the speedometer reads below forty, and everyone who comes by looks over to see if we've got a flat tire or something. Shouldn't we turn back now? Looks like it's going to pour any minute."

"Watch your language!"

Mike wanted to throw up his hands and scream, "Let me alone, let me alone, let me *alone!*" How did anyone *ever* learn to drive? He began to feel that they were going to drive on and on and on and end only with some dreadful catastrophe. There they'd be splattered all over the road with Dad still pointing out everything he'd done wrong. *And* the rain falling in buckets. Dad might want to ignore the weather, but the storm was about to let loose and the *last* place to be in a storm was behind an old man driving an equally old Ford pickup like it was a mule plowing a field. It was too early on Sunday morning for that guy to be drunk so he must be either blind or palsied.

"Mike, don't tailgate that pickup. You're in the clear, pass him. Now. Move out. You can go over forty to pass, for God's sakes. You have to! But don't stay out in this middle lane too long. Now. Switch back to the right lane. Good!"

Mike laughed bitterly.

"What was *that* supposed to mean!"

"It was just that I did something right." They were both quiet. He had been driving for more than half an hour. Pat, had never had him drive so long, and he felt as if he was about to go under. He hunched tight over the wheel. It was getting so dark he could hardly *see* the cars in front, let alone judge distances. They must be hitting the church traffic because there were more cars. And this freeway driving was kill and be killed if you didn't judge your distance right the first time. At least if the wind was steady you could compensate for it and keep in one lane, but these fifty mile an hour gusts that took you by surprise and tried to blow you clear across into the oncoming traffic were something else again. Try to compensate and suddenly there was no wind and you were onto the shoulder. What was it Dad said? The trouble with driving was that you might not get a second chance if you made a mistake. He was so right.

"Dad?"

"Relax, you're doing all right. You don't have to lean out the windshield."

"How about you taking over now, Dad?" Mike

tried to keep his voice steady.

"Not quite yet. You're just getting the feel of it. That's no time to quit."

Want to bet? Mike thought. "It's going to rain," he said aloud. Surely they'd at least get off the freeway if it started to rain.

"If it starts to rain, turn off at the first exit, Mike. But I don't think it will for a while yet." Almost as he spoke, the first thunder plummeted through the black sky. There must have been lightning, though Mike hadn't seen it. The thunder echoed and re-echoed. And then lightning cut through the sky, vibrating over the cars like old-fashioned flicker movies, a nightmare montage of patches of light and black. Suddenly the highway was jammed with cars pushing, honking, cutting in and out, cars gone berserk like birds before a storm, cars trying to get off the freeway or achieve their destination before the deluge broke.

Too late. There were no warning sprinkles. The sky fell. The rain poured down like a waterfall. There must be an exit. He was in the right lane at least. Cars cut in so constantly that he could hardly move, could only see the car in front, instantly supplanted by another and another and another car. There was no room. How could they squeeze in? They were going to crash. There was going to be a terrible crash, one of those thirty-car-each-hitting-the-guy-behind things!

Still no sign of an exit. Mike signaled anyhow.

71

Maybe that would make some guy change his mind about cutting in, make him wait a bit? And it did look like the stream of cars curved. Maybe that was a turn off, maybe just a curve in the highway. It *must* be a turn off. No highway cut down and away like that. Thank God. He couldn't hear a thing with the thunder and rain. Couldn't see anything because the windshield wiper slowed whenever the car did. God, squealing brakes. Somebody got it. More brakes. Poor bastards.

"What the hell do you think you're doing, pulling up on that Chevvie. Just lucky his brakes were good. You could have gotten us both killed. Lord, Mike. As soon as we're off this mess pull over and stop. I'm taking over so we'll get home alive."

Dad was taking over. Thank God. Did *he* cause brakes squealing? But there hadn't been a crash? No, he'd heard no crunching metal, no sirens over the thunder. What Chevvie? He searched the cars ahead and alongside but he could not tell one make from another, not even one color from another in the pelting rain. Not that he was trying to shift blame because maybe he should have made room but he hadn't even seen the car, could not remember it at all. That was the horror! He could have been responsible for the thirty car crash and not even known.

They were moving down the exit now. The cars were still bumper to bumper, and they inched along single file, but it was almost over. No one could cut in here. In a few minutes, surely not more than three or four, Dad would take over. The car in front of him was a maroon Chevvie. Was that the one? Did it indeed manage to cut in or was this just a coincidence, just another Chevvie completely unconnected with that sickening squealing of brakes.

Finally they were driving on a two-lane country road and Mike could pull over to soft dirt. His tires seemed to sigh as he slowed to a stop in the sand. He got out and his legs shook so that he could hardly walk in front of the car and around to the other side. He was as drenched with perspiration under the poncho as he was soaked with rain on the outside. All he wanted was to sit down before he collapsed. He fumbled with the button to open the door and his father reached over and pulled the handle.

"God damn it, at least let me open the door myself!" Mike shouted and slammed the door. "This is the last time I'll ever drive a car with you in it. It's too dangerous."

"That suits me just fine. But don't pull your pet stunt of blaming someone else because you're not the hotshot you thought you were," Dad said as he started the buggy and ground the gears as they spurted out of the sand back onto the road. "Damn thing needs a clutch adjustment."

"Don't alibi," Mike said and couldn't suppress a grin. Even Dad could grind the clutch. Of course, he wasn't used to standard transmissions, but he *had* goofed. Mike pulled a blanket around him. He couldn't seem to stop shaking and it was raining too hard to try putting up the top, which didn't work very well even under ideal circumstances.

"Don't you tell me what to do, young man! You know perfectly well I haven't used a standard transmission in ten years and wouldn't be having to now if you hadn't nearly gotten us and a lot of innocent people killed back there."

"Oh, Lord. Talk about backseat driving," Mike muttered, but fortunately the comment was lost in a roll of thunder. That thunder burst into lightning and more thunder. The rain beat down so hard that Mike stung through his parka. There was no question of talking now. The Grasshopper was awash and buffeted from one side of the road to the other like a rowboat in a squall. Water sloshed above their ankles, around them on the leather seats, drowned them from the skies. They crouched low in a futile search for protection from the lightning, the wind, and the slashing rain. Neither of them said a word. Wasn't it ever going to let up?

After days or hours of a timeless nightmare, they pulled into the outskirts of town. The streets were deserted, all stores and bars were closed. So it was *not* only the fight and the open car and the freeway that made it seem so horrible. It must be a terrible storm if everything was closed. A beach town knows and knows enough to batten its doors and windows against the vindictive collusion of wind and rain and sea.

The car sputtered and threatened to quit as water rejected by the inadequate street gutters splashed into the motor. The middle of Main Street was still passable, but another couple of hours of rain and all streets would be closed. If only the buggy would keep running! This was the first day of winter as far as the town was concerned. It always marked winter not from the solstice but from the first day each year that Main Street flooded.

When Mike and Dad finally pulled into their own driveway and stopped, neither said a word. They climbed out and dashed down the driveway to the front door. Midway Mike saw his mother standing at the window and, veering aside, turned toward the back of the house to his own room, which had an outside entrance. He couldn't face either her or Pat just now. Not yet.

He stripped off his wet clothing and dropped it out on the back stoop. Then he carefully bolted his door, jumped into the unmade bed and pulled the covers up over him. He lay there shivering, still feeling the rain pelting him, hearing the thunder, and the horror of those screeching brakes.

But gradually the quiet in his room grew larger. He began listening to the noises from the rest of the house. Mom was asking Dad if he wanted a little brandy in his coffee. Pat said something he couldn't quite hear.

Either he wanted some brandy too or he was asking Dad about the driving lesson. Well, he'd get an earful if that was it. And trust Pat to listen and not defend him, either! Pat may have said he was ready for a license, but you could bet he wouldn't say so to Dad. And Mom was probably chiming in about how he hadn't made his bed before he left. The indistinct conversation diminished. They must all be in the kitchen eating because he couldn't hear anyone. Probably just as well, but it was sure quiet. He couldn't ever hear the rain on the roof any more.

The worst part of the whole trip was his shattered innocence. He'd actually been looking forward to showing Dad the progress he had made in driving. And he could have if they'd only stayed off that freeway. The basic question was just what made Dad take him on the freeway? Was it to show him, Mike, how stupid he was or because Dad thought he had some deep urge to go strip racing? Neither showed much confidence, considering he'd never brought a major disaster on the Lamons. But none of that was really the worst thing about it. The worst was that now he'd never get Dad to let him drive Mary the six measly blocks to the dance on New Year's Eve. Never in a million years.

It was a long while before Mike stopped quivering enough to face getting dressed. Just how long, he didn't know because his clock had stopped. It said five-thirty. If only that *were* the time and the driving lesson had never occurred. Then he could go out and have breakfast. It must be lunch time because he smelled bacon. Mom knew bacon and tomato sandwiches were his absolute favorite and this must be her subtle way of luring him out. Tough. He just wasn't having any today, thank you. On the other hand, he couldn't very well stay in his room forever.

Just then there was a knock on his door. "Open up, Neanderthal," Pat called cheerfully.

Mike unbolted the door.

"How's the cave, O, Son of Fire?" Pat asked.

"Short on provisions," Mike answered and grinned wryly.

Pat handed him a sandwich, neatly wrapped in a plastic bag.

"The word is that you are to appear for dinner, *en famille*, preferably bearing a white flag. Look, Dad probably shouldn't have taken you out on the freeway and, God knows, not in this weather, but the Driver Training guy threw the fear of God into him by suggesting that you're more concerned about hurt pride than lives, yours or anyone else's. He said you'd rather pass a car than obey the law. That's it, straight, Mike."

Mike flushed darkly. That teacher had been out with him for half an hour, if that, and decided his character for life. And Dad took that gravedigger's word after living with Mike for nearly sixteen years. And what did Pat think? Did Pat share in the general court-martial? They looked at each other. Pat seemed

77

to be waiting for him to say something. He could remind Pat that he'd been telling him what a good driver he was, but they both already remembered that. Or he could agree to come out for dinner and face the music? Or he could force Pat to trust him or show that he didn't? That wasn't fair, but neither was making him a criminal because of one guy's snap judgment.

"Pat, do you trust me?"

Pat nodded, still quiet.

"Then, will you give me the key so I can drive Mary home from the party New Year's Eve?"

"Let's get this straight. You're asking me to break both the law and our joint promise to Dad to prove that you are trustworthy, right?"

"You don't have to get mad. Just say yes or no, Pat."

"And, in spite of taking you out and trying to teach you every day, I'm against you if I don't go back on my word to Dad. Right?"

"He betrayed me," Mike whispered.

"Would you have thought he betrayed you if he'd been pleased with your driving this morning? And *if* he was wrong, doesn't stealing the key jeopardize your right to moral censorship?"

"He decided I was a lousy driver before he even got in the damn car. You just don't understand, Pat. He never treated you this way. And don't try to psych me out of this. You may be my big brother, but you're sure not God!"

"And I know it, which is more than you do," Pat said bitterly and turned to the door. He threw Mike the key and left, closing the door quietly behind him.

Mike stared at the key. It lay on an old Persian rug. He and Pat had bought the rug jointly at an auction four years before and traded it back and forth every six months. This year Pat had given him his interest for Christmas, with a note that he was giving up luxuries for the Spartan life of struggle and study so he could stay in school and out of the infantry. So he was a louse and Pat was suddenly the good example. So what?

Quickly Mike picked up yesterday's pants and shirt from the floor and put them on. He stopped to make his bed and throw Christmas wrappings, presents, and dirty socks in the closet and close the door. Mom wouldn't come into the room for quite a while. That would be violating his privacy, and she'd never like to think she did that.

He sneaked out the back door, over the fence, and headed for town at a dead run.

THE STOLEN KEY

MIKE WAS AFRAID someone might have heard his door slam. He didn't look back. It was absolutely essential that he get to town right away. There was no time to stop for explanations, lunch, making up, or any of the other Lamon family post fight rituals. Fortunately the rain had stopped somewhat short of completely flooding the streets. That was one break. He skirted the major puddles and sloshed through the others, landing knee-deep in mud when he misjudged. No matter. He'd already been wet today.

The important thing was to reach Melgrove's General Store before it closed, if it was open again. Mr. Melgrove closed early on Sundays, sometimes by noon and always in time to make the two o'clock matinee. Today he might not have opened after the storm. But he did like to get every penny he could. One more block would tell if it were shut.

Melgrove's was open and Mike pushed through the last-minute, after-storm shoppers to the back room, which had a butcher shop on one side and some hardware on the other side. Melgrove lost out to the supermarkets during the week, but made up in milk, lunchmeat, and the nail trade after hours and on Sunday.

"Mom wants another key made, Mr. Melgrove," Mike called to the old man behind the butcher counter.

"Sure, go right ahead, kid. You do better keys than me anyhow, and I've got all the earth's customers and then some to take care of this afternoon."

"Sure. Thanks." Mike had hoped he'd be too busy to ask just what key was being duplicated and why. There were times when Mr. Melgrove was the world's nosiest human being and other times when he was the busiest. There seemed to be no middle ground.

Mike twirled the display cone until he caught a dummy that matched and ground the new key. Thirty seconds. Should have thought of this to begin with and saved himself Pat's Sermon. Of course he had to get the key to make the duplicate from, somehow.

Mike measured the two keys to make sure they were exact before he laid the fifty cent piece on the counter and turned to leave.

"Young folks are sure in a hurry these days once they get wheels under them. Can't give a person the decent time of day anymore," Mr. Melgrove muttered behind him. Mike turned and smiled and waved. After all, Mr. Melgrove must be at least seventy. He'd come in and shoot the bull with him next week.

Better not run or someone might notice he was winded and wonder how a football player could lose his breath. Everyone seemed to think he should be an iron man, except Pat who just loved to prove he was a ninety pound weakling at every opportunity. That was one thing about Pat. He sure loved to play knock a guy off the mountain so there was never any question about who was the mighty and generous big brother. He'd better make sure it was the old key he gave big brother. Mike carefully put the shiny new key in his wallet and then sauntered across the vacant lot toward home. After all, he wasn't doing anything to be ashamed of. It *was* his car. He might not ever use the damn key. This was just a good way to let Pat off the hook. Besides, he owed him enough favors already.

Mike still hadn't decided what to do about New Year's Eve when Mary suggested walking. It was *such* a beautiful night she said. That did solve a problem, and he walked with a certain smugness. But as he danced with Mary, the key was in his pants pocket and he could feel it pulsing against his leg. He might not use the key at all, but it was a good security blanket just in case. Mary had said she liked walking in her long dress because it gave people something to think about and it marked this night as special. They weren't just another couple hot rodding to another high school dance.

It didn't look much like the same old high school gym, either. Two hundred live Christmas trees framed the room like a fragrant forest after a rain. That afternoon Mike and all the other lettermen had untrimmed their family trees and hauled them to the gym. Later they'd gone all over town offering to take down a tree if the family would donate it and lend their colored lights to the Letterman's Club for the dance. Christmas was over, needles were falling, and nearly everyone was glad to be rid of his tree so easily. So now they had this forest as full of colored lights as Disneyland.

A thousand balloons and ten dollars worth of serpentine were hidden in fishnets attached to the roof, and at midnight they'd be dropped on the surprised dancers below. The football team had handled decorations, and they were the only ones who knew about the balloons and the serpentine. A twelve man rock-band played in one corner, and a snack bar dispensed food in the other.

Mike had just gotten his varsity letter at the Christmas assembly, so this was the first time he'd ever worked on a dance, gone to a New Year's dance, or worn his letterman sweater. The sweater had been a Christmas present, but he'd saved it for the dance so it wouldn't be torn or dirty. Better be safe than sorry. The boys' white sweaters with red block letters stood out against their girls' brilliant formals and stood out too from the sport coats the other boys wore. Mary's dress was the color of poinsettias, that light fiery red, and it suited her. Hey, it matched his letter. And the color in her cheeks. He'd never seen her so excited, and that was saying quite a lot. Maybe she had never been to a New Year's Eve party before, either.

"I don't know what you're thinking about, but it's sure not the beat," Mary said, jerking her head and shoulders and tapping him on the shoulder to the beat. They were rocking open style and you did have to keep your mind on the music, especially if the whole business of dancing was brand-new.

"I was liking your red dress, if you must know. Your grandfather would tell you it's rude to criticize your date's dancing. I mean, just suppose I got mad and walked off and there you'd be in the middle of the dance floor all by yourself, pouting." Mike grinned. Personally, he didn't think much of a girl who would let her feet get stepped on and not say a word.

"Want to bet?" Mary asked, lifting an eyebrow.

84

"Bet what?"

"That I'd be left all by my poor lonesome like the Statue of Liberty."

"No deal." The stag line had already noticed her. What would she say if he told her that she was all bright and shiny and beautiful like a Christmas ornament? Sounded bad, even to him. Better keep quiet. Better concentrate on the dancing.

"Much better, much better. You must have had more practice than I thought," Mary said, smiling.

Mike laughed joyously. He loved the slight jealousy in her voice, the implication that he'd been around, which was certainly not so.

Mike had worried about the dancing, but when he concentrated they moved well together. He didn't know many steps; Pat had taught him most of the ones he knew during Christmas vacation, but Mary followed so well he stopped worrying and just moved to the music. Whoever thought dancing would be such fun? Dancing with Mary was like running with the ball after you've left the last tackle in the mud. Oh. Oh. Speak of the last tackle and here he came. Trouble Andrews, star tackle of last year's varsity football team. He was bearing down on them like an obsolete battleship.

"Hey, not bad picking for a scrub Sophomore. How about letting the big league take over?" the two hundred and thirty pound alumni asked, tapping Mike on the shoulder. Mike wondered why last year's Seniors always came back to the New Year's dance. It wasn't really for them. Trouble was blond, big rather than fat, and he would have been handsome if it weren't for tiny close-set eyes that gave him a mean and shifty appearance. He was not actually shifty, but he was certainly mean as hell. Trouble had had more fights than all the rest of the team put together; and last year the coach had nearly had heart failure during every game wondering whether Trouble would foul out before they won the game. They'd won the championship last year thanks to Trouble, though. Mike didn't like the big tackle, but he didn't know how he could politely keep him from cutting in on Mary. Fortunately the music stopped and the band leader announced a time out.

"Saved in the nick of time, old buddy. I'll be back, little girl, don't you worry," Trouble said, chucking Mary under the chin.

"Do *that* again, and I'll bite," Mary said seriously.

Trouble raised an eyebrow but said nothing. Nor did he leave. Mike squeezed Mary's hand and was about to ease her off the dance floor toward the snack bar when Trouble put a restraining hand on his shoulder.

"Say—how did your big brother make out with the draft board the other day?" Trouble asked in a tone of voice that indicated he hoped for the worst.

"When?" Mike asked, playing for time. What was he talking about? Pat hadn't been to the draft board lately so far as he knew. His student status wasn't up for renewal yet, was it? It seemed as if they had just gone through all that.

"Three-four days ago. I ran into him and he looked mighty worried, mighty worried. Said they'd revoked his student deferment and he was mighty doubtful about the appeal he was filing, mighty doubtful—but, hell, I'm not telling you no news. How did it go?"

"Why don't you ask *him?*" Mike said and pulled Mary away. He moved blindly, just wanting to get away from that voice, from the reminder that Pat had talked casually about his draft problems with a guy neither of them liked but hadn't mentioned them to his own brother. Dimly he heard Trouble shouting after them to introduce him to his date and warning that he'd be there to claim the next dance. Dimly he heard Mary say she felt she could do quite nicely if she *never* met that bear.

Finding himself at the snack bar he ordered two eggnogs automatically. The last two weeks came crowding back. All the conversations between Dad and Mom and Pat that ended when he entered the room. He'd known something was going on but, egotistically, he'd thought they'd been talking about *him*, about the Grasshopper.

Wow! They weren't talking about him. Probably didn't know he was alive. No wonder Dad hadn't wanted to bother with the driving lesson and exploded so easily when he did go through with it. Why should he have to nurse along a fool fifteen-year-old who wanted to drive when he had serious worries with Pat? Made sense, but why didn't they tell him? Didn't they think he was capable of understanding? God knows he'd never have nagged Pat to go driving with him or to teach him to dance. Why *didn't* Pat tell him? Wasn't he, Mike, a member of the Lamon family, too? It wasn't any state secret if Pat told Trouble, was it?

"Do you think the grizzly bear is telling the truth?" Mary asked gently as they sat on a bench partly hidden in the Christmas trees.

Something's been going on, but I don't understand why no one in my family said anything to me," Mike burst out. He was ashamed to have Mary know that they didn't trust him, but you had to tell someone.

"I know. I mean, that happened to me all the time at home. They thought I was a baby. That's why it's so nice living with Granddaddy. He hasn't anyone but me around so he has to confide in me. He doesn't expect so much, either."

"I'm the youngest so my parents always did treat me like the baby but I'm used to that. It's *Pat!*"

Mary pulled a small branch off a tree and stripped the needles, brushing them off her dress, one by one, thoughtfully. She said nothing.

"I know I've been pretty immersed in myself, with the car and all. And I did know Pat was having a bad time in geometry. He didn't take it in high school and I'm taking it now, so I was helping him with his homework. Doing his homework. He has a mental block about geometry. But they can't take away a deferment because of one course, can they?"

Mary shrugged. "I don't know. That seems ridiculous! But, you know, Pat was talking to my grandfather the other day, and he's awfully proud of you because you do so much better in school than he ever did. Do you suppose—maybe—he hoped if his appeal was granted that he'd never have to tell you how poor his grades were? I mean, especially if you'd been trying to help him and all. I don't know anything about it, really, but—" Mary let the thought trail off.

That made sense. Pat *was* sensitive about his grades. He had been ever since grammar school. Of course, that was Mom's fault. She was a great one for comparing grades—so compulsive about it that Mike remembered hiding his report card so she wouldn't hold him up as a good example to Pat. Pat used to clobber him good for getting better grades back in those days. But would that explain Pat's not talking about losing his deferment? It could be.

"Maybe you're right," Mike said aloud. "I never thought of it that way. But let me tell you about something. Do you remember the first day I ever met you —on the beach? Well, a friend of Pat's had just been drafted, only I didn't know it. We were all lying on the beach and this guy got up and left and no one even said good-bye. I thought maybe everyone was so quiet because they were mad at me. Pat told me about his being drafted later. But it got me, I mean the way no one even said good-bye."

"What did Pat say? Did he say why no one mentioned it?" Mary asked gently.

"He said they might all end up basket cases and the guy deserved one last day at the beach," Mike said, taking Mary's hand.

"I think maybe I'd feel that way too—I mean, lying on the beach with your friends and letting the sun soothe you—I mean, what's better? Anyway, it's not fair, the whole draft law isn't fair. Why do you boys have to be drafted, and all we do is sit around home and *sew?*"

The emphasis on the last word made Mike laugh in spite of himself. It was hard to imagine Mary sewing on a button let alone sitting around the two years he'd be drafted just sewing, sewing, sewing. She wasn't the type. It was easier to imagine her behind the wheel of an Army jeep bouncing through desert maneuvers.

Mike hoped Trouble had found another girl during the intermission. The band was drifting back to the stand. They called themselves the "Royal Tomorrows" and wore purple satin shirts and white levis. They were all up now, a blur of purple and white, checking amplifiers, tuning guitars, kicking instrument cases out of the way. Mike watched them with a certain pride. They'd decided to hire a big band tonight. That meant that in addition to the organ, drums, and guitars, they had a brass sax section. The fuller sound was great. Except when they were tuning up! Tuning up sounded like screeching cats. Finally they were starting. Mike smiled at Mary.

But Trouble had seen the band, too, and he came lumbering across the room, heading right for them. He hadn't forgotten Mary. It wasn't that Mike objected to guys cutting in, but Mary didn't even want to meet this character let alone dance with him. To say nothing of the fact that he'd already done his best to wreck the evening by hashing over Pat's draft status. Why ask except to cause trouble? What was *he* doing at the draft board anyhow? Was Trouble old enough to register? Maybe misery loved company! An interesting thought, but there was no time to waste on abstractions. There had to be some way to get rid of him and fast, because here he came, ready or not.

"Mike?" Mary asked, "do you mind if I duck in the Ladies' Room? I knew I'd rip this dress if I didn't put a gusset under the arm, but I took a chance because I was in such a big hurry to finish this afternoon. Look!"

Mary lifted her arm to show a triangle of white armpit in the red velvet sleeve. Mike stared. So she *did* sew.

"Well?" Mary asked.

"I'm shocked. It's indecent. It's gorgeous. Maybe

Trouble will get lost while you're away. Go, woman!"

Mary drew a spool of thread from her pocket and, holding it aloft, headed for the Ladies' Room. "Tell him I'm *so* sorry," she added just before she disappeared into the crowd, barely in time to avoid Trouble.

"Where is she? Where is she? The band's playing 'Downtown.' That's my music. Got to get with it—where is she?"

Mike nodded towards the Ladies' Room without saying a word. They stood waiting, listening. The band was having a romp. Mike knew they must really like this number. He watched Trouble snapping his fingers, jerking his head and shoulders, not quite keeping up with the rhythm. When the number ended and Mary still hadn't come back, the big hulking tackle narrowed his eyes so they almost disappeared.

"The little bitch. Trying to give us the slip, huh? Well, if she thinks I'm going to hang around waiting for her, she's got rocks in her head. I know where I can get me some real action this New Year's Eve, and it sure as hell ain't at no penny ante high school dance. So long, sucker!"

Trouble stalked toward the door, and Mike thought his retreating back was the happiest sight he'd seen all evening. Mary came out from behind a screen of Christmas trees and held up her arm to prove she had, indeed, mended the dress. Then she tapped Mike on the shoulder.

"Care to dance, mate?" she asked.

"I'm beginning to feel like the center of a whirling dervish," Mike said later. If the music and the dancers kept escalating, the centrifugal force would lift them right off the floor, wouldn't it? Then they could grab the balloons from the ceiling.

"And I was thinking that the Christmas lights are like stars and we were alone in a forest. Only I'd been bewitched and turned into a dune buggy. My poor heart could just pump gas until some handsome prince came along who loved dune buggies enough to kiss one and release me. I saw you walking down this yellow brick road and hope returned for the first time—"

Maybe she meant that he should kiss her? But he hesitated, and it was too late. Another stag cut in and he was back on the sidelines again. Watching. Was she telling her new partner about the wicked enchantment? No. He should probably dance with someone else, just to be nice and to show he could. But it was fun to watch Mary dance and to watch the other guys cut in. She'd wave at him and smile, and when the music stopped, he'd be there to claim her.

It had taken a while for the boys to notice Mary, but once they did she was the most popular girl on the floor. Guys were falling all over themselves coming up to him like old friends and then taking Mary off.

Finally, it was Mary who said enough was enough, and she'd come to dance with her date. After that

Mike just shook his head as the guys with steady girls did, and the disappointed boys would groan or tease and then move on to another girl. It was easy, once you had the knack.

The whole dance was easy once you had the knack. Why had he been so damn worried all week? The big thing was choosing the right girl and, after that, even dancing was a snap. And he'd chosen the right girl. No question there.

He was disappointed when the twelve o'clock whistle blew. So soon? And then they were stomping balloons, throwing confetti, blowing whistles, and kissing everyone in sight. Everyone in the room went berserk! The band played "Auld Lang Syne." Mike stood with his arms around Mary. He didn't want to kiss her now. Everyone was kissing. Just like shaking hands. Later. When they were alone. Maybe out on the dunes. This dance was like Grand Central Station. However, she seemed to be waiting, and if he didn't someone else would. Mike drew Mary gently to him and kissed her. Then he held her, feeling the soft velvet, smelling perfume. Dizzy.

"So, I'm a girl, after all?" She smiled.

"You'd been in doubt?"

"I mean, well—my family always says I'm such a tomboy that no boy would ever feel I was feminine enough *to* kiss me. They said every boy would hand me a wrench instead. Which reminds me, can I help you and Granddaddy put the new generator in the

Grasshopper tomorrow?"

"Mary, you're pulverizing my ego!" Mike threw up his hands in mock horror and kissed her again.

"Yes, Mike?"

"Did anyone ever tell you that you look like a Christmas tree ornament?"

"Santa Claus or Rudolph?"

Then they were in their coats and out the door tasting the cold salt air and the pounding surf instead of a dance band's supplied background music. They cut across frozen empty lots to avoid anyone who might offer a ride, and Mary held her long dress above her knees to keep it off the weeds and grass. At the beach they waded through shifting sand around to the back door of the Varian cabin and stood under the eucalyptus tree.

Mike remembered the eucalyptus covered with Monarch butterflies the day Mary hid the car keys to keep him from buying the buggy, or at least to show him how she felt about it. No butterflies now. And where did butterflies go in the winter?

"Oh, I want to *do* something, something wonderful, wonderful, really crazy!" Mary suddenly shouted, taking Mike's hand and swinging it wide and high.

"Well, you don't have to pull my arm out of its socket," Mike said, feeling for the key in his pocket. There it was, and they could take off with one turn of the ignition. Still he hesitated. "Like what, Mary, like what?" he asked.

"Oh, how do I know? I just want to *do* something! Don't you ever feel that way, Mike?"

Sure he felt that way sometimes. Now. That was why he'd made the key. He'd been mad at Dad too, but that wasn't the main thing. He wasn't mad now. But the Grasshopper was his, and he should be able to take a ride if he wanted. Mike took the key out of his pocket and held it in front of Mary. It glimmered in the moonlight. They both looked at the key for a moment, and then Mike laid it in Mary's hand and closed her fingers over it. He hoped she didn't notice how new and shiny this particular key looked.

"The car's here, and I don't need a license to drive on the dunes," he said. He watched Mary closely. She seemed to be considering. Lord knew, he didn't want to force her to go for a ride. They *could* walk. This had been too good a date to spoil. Finally Mary smiled and it was like somebody turning on the light.

"Can I say what we do?" Mary asked.

Mike knew he should ask why. There was something about the way she asked that spelled trouble. No, not trouble, but problems.

"Please?"

"Sure, just name it," Mike replied, still dubious. But, after all, what could she want?

"Lovely. You're just lovely, you know that, Mike. Let's go hunt arrowheads on the Indian shell mounds in the dunes. Granddaddy says the obsidian shows up more against the white clam shells in the moonlight."

"At one in the morning?" Mike exploded. He might have known. What a goofy idea. There was something about graveyards at night, even if they were Indian graveyards that hadn't been used for over a hundred years, that was a little weird. He and Pat both had their collections of the obsidian arrow and spearheads that they found on the great dune shell mounds. Every dune bum did. But at night?

He'd found a skull there more than once, and that was sure not the perfect way to end this date. The shell mounds were originally places the Indians deposited clam shells from feasts, but some were also burial mounds. Even with the shifting sands of a hundred years, half a hundred of these mounds were still around. The stories of ghosts were pretty persistent. They were supposed to roam at night. Even the dune rider clubs cut a wide path around shell mounds at night.

"What's wrong? You afraid of Injun Joe?" Mary teased.

Injun Joe was supposed to roam the dunes at night looking for the white man who cut off his head a hundred years ago. There'd been a price on Joe's head, so the story went, because he had killed the man who stole his wife. Of course, ghosts weren't true, but why tempt the fates?

"Oh, Mike. Injun Joe is straight out of *Tom Sawyer*."

"Just 'cause the name's the same? This Joe *did* live

97

here." But why make a big thing of it. They could go for a ride and he'd make Mary forget all about arrowheads. It should be the easiest thing in the world to convince her that they'd ride tonight and come back tomorrow to look for arrowheads. Mike smiled confidently.

"Bring on Injun Joe! I only hope you don't look like his long lost wife!"

"Might be interesting." Mary winked as Mike opened the car door in honor of her long dress. It was still there by the house where Pat had left it when they decided to walk. He hoped Mary's grandfather didn't hear the engine.

"Lucky that once Granddaddy is asleep even a tidal wave couldn't wake him," Mary said. She slid the key into the ignition.

The Grasshopper started right off. Lucky! Lately they'd been having trouble because the car needed a new generator, the one Mary wanted to help install tomorrow. That was why Pat decided to leave the car, so he wouldn't have to get up in the morning. Pat would have a fit if he ever heard that he, Mike, had kissed Mary and then she had asked to help install the generator. He'd die laughing. Mike blushed.

They rolled almost noiselessly down the driveway and off the road to cut between the first dunes, past pungent sage and past lupine bushes popping their dry pods like firecrackers announcing the New Year. The night was cold, cloudy, and still. The slowly moving car scarcely ruffled the sand on the quiet dunes. Even the surf was gentle, sliding onto the beach a little farther with each wave. There were no lights except those on the buggy and the stars. Good thing he had his beacon on, even though it was hard on his already low battery. It hung fifteen feet up from the car on a bamboo pole so another dune rider could see them coming over a dune.

Mike parked on the crest of a high dune overlooking the ocean. Fortunately there was no wind. He'd have to retrace the tracks to find his way back to the cabin. The tide was coming in too fast to count on running back along the beach. The dunes where they rode, were set back from the ocean about a hundred yards and ran about three miles wide and ten miles long and they all looked alike in the moonlight. It was a great place to get lost.

Mary craned her neck, looking around. Her face looked pale under the moonlight and her half-smile was impish.

"Where's the shell mound?" she asked.

"Near," Mike said. He turned Mary's face gently and kissed her. This time the kiss was all he'd hoped it would be. But when he tried to kiss her again, Mary drew away.

"*Basta*," she said.

"Mary, you're beautiful," Mike replied and put his arm back around her shoulder and kissed her fluffy hair gently. Then he heard a sharp metallic click. The next thing he knew the car door was open and Mary had slipped out, stumbled into the sand and, picking up her long skirt, run behind the next line of dunes.

Mike was stunned. He just sat. Then he tumbled out of the car.

"Mary, come back here. Mary? Mary, where the hell are you?"

TERROR AT
BARBECUE FLATS

SHE WAS GONE. Vanished into thin air. Mike listened
for some clue, but he heard only the rising sea and,
far off, the cry of the mockingbird. Clouds had rolled
over the moon so he could not even find her footsteps
in the thickening darkness. Suddenly a shrill whining
howl shattered the still night. How close was that
damn coyote? Was there going to be an answer? How
many were there? A pack would attack a lone human.
Did Mary even know coyotes hunted the sand dunes
in packs? And Pat said someone had seen mountain
lion tracks around. They came down once in a while

when food was scarce on the mesa. And it was scarce this winter, this coldest winter in how many years did Dad say? Twenty-three? Where was she? She must be freezing to death if nothing worse.

So, what happened, anyhow? Mary wasn't the type to run away from a kiss. She *would* take off if she knew he didn't plan to hunt her precious arrowheads. But she didn't know. And, besides, he'd hunt the damn things if it meant all that much. It would sure be easier to face Indian Joe than to hunt her all over the Sahara.

Suppose she'd picked midnight on the dunes for a little game of hide and seek? After all, she'd played that game before, only with a certain key. So what was he supposed to do, count to five hundred and come looking? Damned if he would! He'd just sit and wait for her to come back on her own little feet.

Mike pulled his poncho out of the back seat and dropped it over his head. He jerked a navy cap over his ears and squatted on the sand in front of the car. The bumper cut into his ribs when he leaned back. The sand blew into his eyes and mouth. Why didn't that damn coyote shut up? Was it one or two? Never mind. Somebody had to call her bluff. She'd be back soon—unless—she was lost and couldn't find her way back?

"Mary? Mary! Alle, alee, all come free! Please, Mary!" Mike shouted at the top of his lungs. He stood up and looked around. It was as if he were in a canyon on the moon. Every dune looked alike and the shadows seemed to keep moving them around as if they were part of a light show. It was eerie and menacing, as if they were moving toward him. "Mary, please," he called again.

"Mike? Yoohoo! I'm over here. In the cove the dune riders call Barbecue Flats. I found the shell mound. I wanted to bring you an arrowhead so *bad* but I can't even find one," Mary yelled.

"What in hell for?" Mike yelled back. What a relief. Wouldn't you know? Any other girl would be cold and frightened, but Mary was out hunting for arrowheads.

"For a New Year's present, silly."

Lord. And what did she expect him to do, send her roses by camel?

"I'm sorry, Mike."

"Well, where are you?" Mike skirted around the dune toward her voice. Suddenly he stepped into nothing and tumbled head over heels down a twenty foot cliff of soft sand. Sand in his eyes, sand in his mouth, sand in his hair and clothes. He landed with a thump at the foot of the dune, right in front of Mary.

"Humpty-Dumpty," he said.

"Oh, are you all right?" Mary asked, helping him up.

"I forgot these shadows can fool you at night," Mike explained shaking himself to let the sand fall through. "Yeah, arms and legs all work."

"Are we friends, then?" Mary asked, beginning to giggle.

"Even you would lose your cool—sure, we're friends," he answered, laughing with her. When Mary laughed, her whole face had such happiness you couldn't help but go along with it. Besides, she was so beautiful in that long red velvet against her white face and the whiter dunes. Made her dark hair look like a halo. Maybe that was stretching it a bit but not too much.

"I know what you mean about shadows," she said. "There's something psychedelic about the moving shadows on the sand and the clouds in the black sky."

"Well, it leaves me cold."

"Actually, it *is* kind of spooky. At least when the dune rider club camps here, there are lots of people. What's that?" Mary asked grabbing Mike.

"Only toads, a big old chorus of toads. Must be fresh water close by, probably over under that clump of willows. The Indians always had their clambakes near an oasis." Mike tried to sound casual, but the toads had given him a turn too. How come they suddenly started gargling then?

"Oh, I want to go see them."

Mike looked around carefully. He didn't want to go climbing over any more dunes with shifting shadows than he could help. Nor did he want to move any farther from the car. All they needed was to lose the car. The Indian shell mound spread up the side of the dune facing them. The toads must be over under the willows. Let them have the willows and the snakes and raccoons, too.

"Over in the willows. But I'd hate to wake anything larger that lives in there. I'd even hate to wake a rattlesnake. Why don't we stick to the arrowheads?" Hunting arrowheads was about the safest thing that seemed to interest Mary tonight.

The moon came out as they started up the long gradual sweep of sand. The shells were bright white. Mr. Varian was right. Anything atypical did show up better than by daylight. Still, Mike couldn't get over the feeling that they had no right to be there at night. It was a crazy feeling. After all, why were they intruders more by night than by day? But he couldn't help it. There were bones scattered among the shells. Some were obviously rabbit or raccoon or large fish, but what were the others? Rabbit and raccoon tracks crisscrossed the mounds. Mike felt a cold blast of wind cut across his back. He shivered. Mary pressed his hand. "You must really be freezing," he said, putting one arm around her bare shoulders.

"Hmmm," Mary replied. "Do you think we're ever going to find anything—"

Suddenly she knelt and began digging furiously in the sand with her bare hands, spewing sand in all directions.

"Hey, what did you find?" Mike asked.

Mary didn't answer. She kept digging. Finally she lifted out a large dark conical object. "Only a big old abalone shell," she said throwing it down in disgust. "I thought I'd found a bowl. Damn."

"They did use abalone shells for bowls," Mike said soothingly.

But Mary was no longer listening. She was staring toward the top of the dune.

"Oh, no," she whispered, grabbing Mike and pulling him down to the ground with her.

Mike looked up and froze too. Two coyotes stood silhouetted against the night sky. Their eyes shone like red coals and they were staring straight at Mike and Mary. They stood taut and ready to jump—toward them or to run away?

"Shhhhhhhh," Mike whispered, crouching against the cold sand.

A piercing howl filled the night and settled in the marrow of his bones. When it was over, even the toads were silent. Only the wind and the lap of the ocean broke the terrible stillness. Surely two coyotes wouldn't attack! But maybe the howl was a call for reinforcements. There were tales of a pack attacking men and tearing them to shreds. What could he tell Mary? They had no weapons of any sort. All they could do was run, and coyotes were supposed to run faster than cars. If they could only reach the car. Of course, maybe the coyotes were scared too. Maybe they'd run away.

Mike looked up to the top of the hill again. No, they were still there, the skinny overgrown sheep dogs with the bushy fox tails and those terrible red eyes. They were still staring, hypnotized. And so was Mary. Her eyes, widened like saucers, were fixed on the coyotes, holding their eyes in some awful stare-down. Nothing had changed, but this couldn't go on forever.

"Let's get out of here before any more come. I don't think two will attack," Mike said with more conviction than he felt.

"You mean, run?" Mary asked in amazement.

"Back to the car. We don't have any weapons so it's our only—I mean our best chance."

"I've heard that fire or banging tin pans scares them," Mary whispered, still staring at the eyes.

"Neither of which we have."

"I know. Shall I take the abalone shell?"

"Sure, at least we can throw it. Better than nothing. Wait until they howl again if we can. Maybe they won't be watching us then."

The long bloodcurdling howl started again, like a series of high pitched fog horns.

"Now!" Mike ordered and they stumbled up the dune. Damn the sand. Damn the coyotes. Mike kicked off his shoes. How could Mary run in that long dress? The car was just over the crest of the dune. Just keep going. Mike looked at Mary and saw that tears were streaming down her face. But she kept up.

There was another howl. Good. At least they weren't on top of them. It sounded as if they hadn't moved. There was no time to look back and see. At last! They made the lip of the dune and sank into the sand. Falling on their knees, they crawled over the dune and headed down for the car. Thank God the top was up. It should be *some* protection.

Mike didn't stop for anything until they were both in the car and the doors were locked. Then he turned and looked out the back window. There were no coyotes in sight. Mary was still crying, gulping, trying to stop, looking out the window too.

"None?" she asked.

"None. They probably turned and ran the opposite way just as fast as we did," he said feebly, uncertainly.

"Those terrible red eyes!"

And those lean ribs sticking out as if they were saying *hungry, hungry* Mike thought. There was no question of going back over the dune even if they could find the way and even if they were in a car and even if coyotes didn't usually attack men. They'd have to chance it going home by the beach, rising tide or not. What time was it?

Another howl cut through the night. It was only the foghorn. But fog coming in and the tide coming in at the same time was double trouble. "Mary, what time is it?"

"Almost two. Oh, Mike, those awful awful red

eyes. And he was licking his chops. Did you see how long his tongue was? I'll never come back to Barbecue Flats as long as I live. Never. Never. Never."

"Two? You're kidding! We've got to get out of here. We'll have to go along the beach even with the tide coming in. Can't risk meeting the pack on the dunes. No, don't worry. We won't." And silently Mike hoped they weren't too late.

"You forgot the lights," Mary said when they were ready to start.

"Can't use them. The battery's too low. Have to start the car first," Mike said as he turned the key in the ignition. The starter growled, growled again and almost caught, so close you couldn't imagine that it did not. Next time. Next time wasn't even close. Mike switched off the key. It didn't sound good. Wait a minute. Now, again. The growl was low and feeble. He'd better quit while he was ahead, while the engine responded at all. All right, he knew the generator was kapooey but it had started like a dream an hour before. Don't stop now, he prayed, not now with coyotes gathering forces over the dunes and the tide coming in on the beach and Dad waiting up at home. Please, not now, Mike begged as he tried once more. Nothing.

"Want me to man the ignition while you fiddle with the engine like I used to do for Grandpa?" Mary asked.

"Wouldn't help. Because we've got both battery

and generator troubles. Your Granddad told me that if he could get the battery water moving sometimes that helped, but it wouldn't help now with the generator gone too. Damn, maybe if she weren't cold—I think we're going to have to push her over the ridge and try to start in compression. O.K.?" Mike tried to sound sure, but he wished he knew more about what actually went on inside a motor. Maybe he should have listened to Dad's lectures on mechanics. He knew the battery and the generator had to cooperate and in his car neither was doing its part, but how, how the hell, did the process go?

"Without lights?" Mary asked.

"They probably wouldn't go on, even if we tried. Are you afraid, Mary? I sure got us in a mess." She must be thinking lights would keep off the coyotes.

"Just of getting you in trouble. It isn't fair if you don't get home or flip over the car just because I wanted to hunt arrowheads. Mike—do you think maybe we should just leave the Grasshopper and come back and get her in the morning?"

"We can't. We can't risk meeting a pack of you know what. Besides, I guess I might as well tell you. I got mad at Dad—with good reason, but this isn't the time or place for the whole gory story of my driving lesson. Anyhow, as a result I got an extra key made at the general store so I could drive you to the dance tonight without permission. So, if we don't get this car home tonight, I may as well give up driving until

I'm twenty-one because Dad would never get over my breaking a rule, never." Well, Mike thought, she knew the worst now. Here she was with an incompetent thief, in the middle of the Sahara Desert being pursued by wild animals.

"Maybe we could get up at five and at least start her by daylight. No, I guess they'd catch us when they got up for breakfast. It'd be just our luck to have everyone get up early. Well, let's go. I don't think I could start in compression so is it O.K. if I just push? And Mike, it was just great of you to risk all that just for me."

Actually, Mike thought, it hadn't been getting to the dance so much as getting even with Dad, but if that made stealing O.K. he wasn't going to labor the point. Thank God, Mary was willing to push. It didn't seem right to suggest that a girl push but, on the other hand, he probably knew the car better than she did and *would* have more chance of getting it started. He could help push, too, until they reached the lip of the dune. Mike let out the brake and set the gear in neutral. They both hopped out. Mary fell naturally into the rhythm he set. The buggy was five feet from the crest when he jumped back in. The car slowed. Mary gave an enormous shove, then another. He was over. Halfway down to the gully and the engine still hadn't caught. Then, all at once, there it was. A sputter. A pop.

"Hoorray!" Mary yelled.

"Save your breath and run. Can't stop. I have to get up this rise. Come on."

"Just keep gunning, Commodore. I'll catch up. Don't worry about me."

She runs like a kangaroo, Mike thought, as he saw Mary dashing down one dune and then hopping up the forty-five degree dune he was on. He didn't dare slow down with the engine sputtering as if every revolution were its last, but if he ever got to the crest and it was still running, he would run like a snail so she would have a chance to catch up. This was *one* date she'd remember, whether she wanted to or not.

The Grasshopper was coming close to the crest of the dune. The moment of truth was arriving, that moment when the car either made it over the knife edge lip of sinking shifting sand or conked out. He'd watched dune buggy races a hundred times and knew that eighty percent conked out. And they were in real trouble if the motor died on *this* particular crest because it fell off into a giant sand trap and he'd never be able to spring them.

"Make it, make it! Please. Up and over, easy does it, just a little more and we can ride along the crest until we find an easy slope to the beach and then I can take Mary home. All's well that ends well. Don't buck like that. Don't. Up and out of the sand, please, old buggy," Mike gently coaxed his car. He felt his rear wheels spinning, spitting back fantails of sand, but the motor was still running. As long as there was noise there was hope. The tires were cross-notched so they shouldn't sink back if he could just keep going, just make that last lunge over the top. Damn that generator. Would have put in a new one today if he hadn't been running all over town collecting old Christmas trees. Damn old Christmas trees. Oop, the engine missed a beat, and so did his heart. Mt. Everest, here we come, up and over the top.

"You made it! Hip, hip hooray!" Mary yelled, leaping in the sand pit behind him. He could have backed right into her if those tires hadn't held. Ugh. But they had.

He ran as slowly as possible along the level crest. It was matted with sand verbena so traction was good. About time they got a break. And the moon was out, finally. Mary should be able to catch up before he had to make any more decisions.

"Be with you in a minute," Mary gasped with what sounded like her last breath. She pulled alongside and grabbed hold of the door. Mike reached over and took her arm.

"Wait until I say ready and then I'll jump and you haul," she gasped.

"O.K."

"All right. Ready!" Mike pulled and Mary catapulted into the buggy. She was barefoot. The buggy swerved, but Mike brought it back under control. Mary lay back exhausted, her breathing heavy.

"Glad to have you aboard, Mate," Mike grinned,

"but what happened to your shoes?"

"Did you ever try to cross the desert in a pair of baby dolls? I hate shoes, anyhow. You should talk. You left yours for the coyotes." She giggled. "Hey, we did it. *We did it!* Good old little green Grass-hopper. Good old Mike and good old me! Do you believe we actually putted out of that sand trap! Hey, you don't seem overjoyed—what's wrong?"

"Nothing, nothing, so far. It's just that I can't see these damn dips five feet ahead and one slip and we're over the side. But it looks like this ridge *may* lead down toward a sand wash that *may* lead to the beach if we are just phenomenally lucky. Can you see what I mean?"

"Unfortunately, yes."

They both peered into the shadows for driftwood, oil cans, a dead bird, a clump of seaweed, tumbleweed, or any of the other beach clutter that could cause them to slip from their precarious perch. Below them lay the beach, ocean, and maybe safety. If this were daylight or their own lights worked, they could ride down any dune. But in the dark, even with the half-glow of a moon, the situation was tricky, and Mike knew that he must wait for the clear path of a sand wash. He didn't have experience enough to risk flip-ping the car in a gully. But it did look like their crest led down a wash that might run out to the beach. It must be a dune rider trail because there were green marker flags indicating a safe trail for dune buggies.

"Fasten seatbelts. Here we go, Mary! Watch out for driftwood below."

"Aye, aye, sir."

They started down. At first there was just sand under the wheels but soon Mike felt a crunching, like breaking glass. What now. The moon was gone too. Cautiously, he looked over the side. Shells. Thousands of clam shells spread out on every side of them.

"Oh, it's only another Indian shell mound," Mary sighed.

"I feel as if I'm pulverizing history, but there's no way out now. Look out for driftwood. We can't stop for arrowheads."

"How about Indian Joe?" Mary laughed.

"He can help push."

"Mike, don't worry about the shell mounds. If they've lasted a hundred years through the wind storms we have in this neck of the woods, they'll survive your buggy. Oh, oh. Part of a telephone pole down left."

"O.K. got it," Mike said, swerving the car around the driftwood pole.

Neither spoke again until they reached the beach. There Mike ran the buggy down to the hard sand and cruised a few feet above the debris line, where a tangle of shell and algae and seaweed lay in the convolutions of the tide. The tide was rising all right and it would already be too high for conventional tires but the airplane tires on this popcorn machine should make it.

Even with the dune buggy they didn't have much more than half an hour's grace because the creek between them and home would soon be too high to cross.

But they'd probably make it home now. There might be a reception committee of outraged parents waiting, but at least they had escaped the coyotes and made it out to the beach with a dying generator. That was something, after all. He might not be the best driver in the world, but even the prophet of the marble orchard would have to admit he'd come through tonight. Even Dad. Mike put one arm loosely around Mary's shoulder.

"Warm enough?" he asked.

"Don't distract me. I'm watching for driftwood." She laughed and pulled his poncho around her. "I never knew the night ocean was so black and quiet and—gentle. Is it always like this?"

"Usually. Not in a storm, of course. I'm glad you like it, Mary, because it means a lot to me. Some people hate the ocean. Take Pat. He calls the ocean the green octopus. He avoids it like the plague. He's always been leery of it."

"Did he nearly drown or something? I always think it's like a blanket, a big fluffy comforter."

"You wouldn't if you went swimming about now. It's freezing," Mike said. He didn't want to talk about Pat and drowning. Pat's fear was real and worrying in a way he couldn't explain.

"Besides, I wouldn't want to be late getting home."

Mike groaned. "And how are we going to sneak you in?"

"I have a plan. Once we get in the driveway couldn't you cut the engine and we could push the buggy back where she was and I can just go on in the back way. And hope that my dear grandfather isn't waiting at the kitchen table with a rolling pin."

Mike hoped that Pat and his father were not waiting with rolling pins either. It would be three before he got home. There were already beads of dew on the sand. Suppose Pat decided to come in for a chat and found him gone? Suppose Mom and Dad decided to pop in and ask whether he had had a good time? They made a point of not waiting up for Pat, but there hadn't been enough occasions when they didn't have Mike in by 10 P.M. to know how they'd behave. He was the baby, after all, and not to be credited with the good sense of the firstborn. And, if they caught him tonight, they wouldn't trust him again until he was thirty at least.

"You don't think they'd take away the Grasshopper, do you, Mike?"

"Probably. But think positively. Maybe we won't be caught. Here we go."

They turned in the driveway and Mike cut the engine. The silence was deafening. Mike heard every cricket, owl, creaking board and even someone's snores, all simultaneously. If Mr. Varian was waiting up, he'd turned off the lights. Maybe he'd gone to Mike's house to alert his parents. No, his motorcycle was sitting on the porch.

The moon had gone behind another cloud so it was pitch black, and they couldn't see a foot ahead. All they'd have to do to get caught was run over a cat's tail and have it yowl. Or wake a dog, any dog.

"It ought to be O.K. right here," Mike whispered.

"Was that where you had it?" Mary asked dubiously.

"Um-hm." Mike reached for Mary and kissed her. "May as well be hung for a sheep as a lamb," he said.

"Goodnight, Mike. I had a wonderful time." She grinned over the standard end-of-date words, and Mike laughed gently.

"I'll wait."

"You turn right around and run for it, now. You play your lottery, and I'll play mine. We'll compare notes in the morning. Now *go!*" Mary said as she headed for the back door.

AN
IMPORTANT CHOICE

MIKE KNEW he couldn't complain about the family
prying into his date. Either they didn't know what
time he got in, or they were showing a rare understanding. Or Pat had gotten in so much later that
he lucked out by comparison. Dad had asked Pat
whether the dawn was spectacular, and Pat had just
laughed and said that with so many of his friends
already in the draft, those that were left had to celebrate for them, too. And Dad hadn't said one more
word. He had even looked kind of guilty. About
what? Strange. Personally, Mike thought Pat used

the draft to get his own way in everything. He had Mom and Dad walking on eggs. Anyhow, it had been lucky for *him*, and breakfast had been an unusually pleasant meal. The Lamons traditionally ate steak and french fries on the first morning of the New Year because Mom hoped this would keep the family "beefed up" and healthy the rest of the year.

Maybe it was the good breakfast or maybe you just didn't feel tired right away after a late night, or maybe it was just good to have a sunny day in January. Whatever the reason, Mike had a definite feeling that he was starting the year right as he cut across vacant lots still white with frost toward Mary's house. He carried the new generator for his car in a double gunny sack slung over one shoulder. From time to time he shifted the burden. Even twenty pounds could get heavy after half a mile or so.

Finally, he was almost to the cluster of beach cabins, bait houses, bars and clam fork and motorcycle rental places that made up the Varians' neighborhood. He wondered if the motorcycle rental shop was open on New Year's day and if Pat had to work. He hadn't said anything about it. All Pat did was check kids in and out on the Hondas and sit around talking with Mary's grandfather most of the time. Talk about soft jobs.

Mike turned in the gravel driveway under the purple bougainvillea vine. There was his green buggy looking just as innocent as if it hadn't conked out last night. There was Mary's grandfather sitting in the morning sun reading the paper as usual. He sure didn't look as if he knew about last night. Not that he'd probably alter his schedule even if he *did* know. Mary said you could bake a cake by the regularity with which her grandfather read the morning paper between 8:45 and 9:30. It came after breakfast and dishes and before his morning walk.

If Mr. V. didn't get mad and they didn't need any other parts, the year would be off to a fine start. They'd better not need any more parts because no auto parts or hardware store in the whole country would be open on New Year's Day. Besides, the generator had taken his last twenty bucks and getting a new battery would take the next twenty he earned. You had to pick a lot of prickly artichokes in ankle-deep mud to earn twenty dollars in the winter. That popcorn machine would have him in the poorhouse, would have already if Mr. Varian hadn't offered to help repair her.

"Hi, ready to go to work, Mr. Varian?" Mike asked tentatively. No use acting guilty until you were accused.

"Good morning, Mike. Happy New Year. Catch your limit of clams already?"

Mike set down the gunny sack with a clunk. "Very funny! You know darn well that I caught this generator by picking artichokes one whole week of Christmas vacation. Weighs about the same as a sack of clams, though. Heavy as sin."

"That's an interesting comparison," the prospector said, folding his newspaper neatly.

What was that supposed to mean? Was he talking about last night? If only Mary would come on out and give him the word. Mike looked through the open door into the kitchen-living room but there wasn't any sign of her. She was probably still asleep.

"By the way, just in case you were hunting for Mary. She's not here," Mr. Varian said in an offhand manner.

"What do you mean, not here?" Had she been afraid to go in last night? What had happened? Where was she?

"Don't blow a gasket now."

"But where is she?" Maybe they'd had a fight, and she ran away.

Mr. Varian shrugged. "By now I reckon she's down at the gym cleaning up last night's mess for you."

Mike looked closely at Mr. Varian. The old man was grinning. Sitting in the sun making fun of him. It was going to be like pulling teeth finding out about Mary, but at least she was O.K. What a tease he was.

"No, I mean really," Mike persisted. He might as well play the game.

"Really. The cleanup committee apparently went by your house and came on here, and Mary said she'd be noble and go in your place so you could work on the buggy this morning."

"Was one of the guys named Trouble?" Mike asked abruptly.

"Not that I remember. Speaking of names, though, I have a favor to ask of you, Mike. One of the advantages of prospecting as a way of life is we never stand on formality. Never could see the sense of it. Would it offend your sense of respect due an old man if you were just to call me Peter? Every time I hear Mr. Varian I look around quick to see if my old preacher grandpa is back checking up on me. Please?"

He smiled, and Mike thought there was something very sad in his smile. Maybe Mr. Varian felt bad about being old. He never complained or talked about his health like other old people but he must be lonely. His wife was dead; and when Mary's family came back from Iran, he'd be all alone again. Mr. Melgrove, in the grocery store, was always insulted if Mike didn't stop to talk a bit, and then spent the time complaining about how busy he was. He was old, too. Maybe he *needed* to be busy.

"Thanks Peter. I did feel a little left out when I heard Pat calling you Peter and I had to say Mr. Varian, as if you didn't approve of me or something." Mike grinned and hoped Mr. Varian hadn't noticed the slight hesitation before he answered. "I sure hope Mary didn't get stuck with Trouble this morning. He was kind of sore because she didn't dance with him last night." Mike hurried on because he was concerned, and also because he wanted to get away from the name business, which was embarrassing.

"She liked the people she went with, two boys and three girls, if I remember correctly. Don't worry, Mike. Mary has a good head on her shoulders and she only goes where she wants to."

"Well, she sure didn't get much sleep," Mike grumbled.

"That so?" Peter lifted one eyebrow. There he went putting his foot in his mouth again. Now Mr. V. would ask, casually, about what time they did get in. Or perhaps he already knew.

"She left this here for you, incidentally. Consolation prize, I reckon."

The old prospector tossed Mike a five pound salt sack filled with sand. What the hell was that? Mary's sense of humor again? Mike felt something working down to the bottom of the sack. A key? *The* key! It must be! Had he left it in the ignition or dropped it somewhere? Lord, the car could have been stolen. Mike couldn't remember pulling the key out of the ignition. Had Mary or had her grandfather found it? He ripped open the note. Whew! *She'd* found it.

"The luck of the Irish, and you needn't think you'll ever live to forget it," the note said. Mike blushed, folded the note gently and tossed the sand sack onto the front seat of the Grasshopper. He glanced sharply at Mr. V. as the key gave a dead clunk on hitting the floor. But he had the back up and was busy examining the engine.

"Let's get the show on the road. I aim to finish up in time for my afternoon nap, my concession to being an old man. How's that for a New Year's resolution?"

Peter Varian was a careful workman, and he had prepared Mike for his first work on the car. He'd given him a repair manual and told him to memorize it. None of the Lamon men had ever been particularly mechanical and so this repair job would be learning about the insides of his car for the first time. It was a lot like human anatomy, really, if you thought of your heart as a pump, for example.

There was no question that Peter loved motors. His blue eyes gleamed as he outlined the functions of the generator. The generator, as he told it, furnished the power to run the battery so if it was faulty even a small drain like turning on the lights would wear down the battery. It *might* mean only worn out brushes, and those could be replaced. But changing the generator brushes could mean more work than replacing the whole part and there was also the probability that in a week or a month something else in the generator would give. Therefore, you might as well do the thing right and change the whole generator while you had your hands in the grease. This usually saved money and time in the end. While they had the hood up, he finished, they might as well see to the little slip in the fan belt and clean up the points. Preventive medicine.

"Now you do the dirty work and I'll play straw

boss," he said, stepping aside. "That's the way you'll get to know this little buggy. All right. Easy does it. One more twist and the fan belt should slip right off. Don't have to take the fan all the way off to slip out the generator but it's just as easy. Am I driving you bugs peering over your shoulder?" He laughed as he shook back his mane of white hair.

"No, I just pretend you're a famous heart surgeon with a broken hand." Mike grinned.

"Just for that crack I'm going to tell you how I got a broken hand once and, as a result, how I started using a car for prospecting instead of a donkey. You know, lots of prospectors *still* use donkeys. Look at *Death Valley Days* and you think a donkey is the *only* way. Course some men don't use anything but their feet. Lots of damn fools in any way of life but prospecting has more than its share.

"Well, I was still a young man then and Mary's grandmother and I, we'd gone up to the Mother Lode country to try our luck. Everyone goes there eventually to see if he can't outguess the forty-niners and find the golden city. It's like winning the Kentucky Derby or the Irish Sweepstakes to find a rich stake in the Mother Lode, or that's what we thought. Now I know it's the pot at the end of the rainbow—a shimmery mirage.

"But those were depression days in the thirties, it was spring, and we were both punch drunk with my quitting farming and taking up a wandering life. Even then I knew better than to make gold my main object, and we'd done fairly well on the semiprecious stone trail—found some turquoise and a hillside of amethyst, damn near. But gold has a special lure, no sense denying it, and we'd made enough cash to take a flyer.

"So we had these two donkeys, Shorty and Jerry, and we started out. Guys in cars, Model A Fords mostly because they could take off from the road near as well as your buggy, would pass us, but I'd feel superior 'cause we were off the track with a donkey and might find the strike they'd pass by at twenty miles an hour. A mule seemed more professional for a prospector.

"Well, there's an old wives' tale that some donkeys can scent gold and silver. I'd paid an extra thirty dollars for Jerry because he was supposed to have the scent. Man who owned him before has one of the richest silver mines in the state now.

"Anyhow, Jerry started acting funny about two weeks out. Sniffing like crazy. Braying in the night. We kept them tied on a fifty foot tether and he even chewed through that. I cursed the noise but, still, I gave him his lead every morning, and every day my hopes got higher. He'd sniff around, snort, and take off like a house afire. *He* knew where he was going. That was plain.

"Mary's grandmother thought we'd be better off following the geological map I'd drawn up that showed a spot where the conditions might be right for a vein of gold. But she generally gave me my lead too, and so we took off after Jerry.

"We had followed that donkey nearly a week when one morning we woke up and Jerry was gone. Just plain gone. Shorty looked as bewildered as we did, but she was a dumb old thing, anyhow. Our divining rod had vanished. I could have sat down and cried! But instead I yelled and yammered and hunted around. About feeding time Jerry came back, looking pleased as punch. I could have killed him but, of course, I wanted that strike. The next morning he didn't want to go anywhere, just sat down, period. We never did get started that day. The next day he ran off again but this time I followed him—right smack up to a damn female donkey in heat. And that's what I'd been following!

"As if I didn't feel fool enough, when we got back to town the big talk was about a guy who made a strike, not rich but good—right where my map figured gold should be. Well, I gave that damn donkey away to the man who told me about it, and the next morning Mary's grandmother and I walked out to Placeville and ordered a Ford sent up on the next train from San Francisco. To this day I can't stand the sight of a donkey. Something downright sneaky about them," the prospector added, reaching for the grimy old generator that Mike handed him.

"Don't see how you can blame Jerry for doing what came naturally." A voice behind them spoke and then laughed.

"Well, Mr. Lamon, sir, Happy New Year! Shouldn't be surprised if we make a first rate mechanic of your boy, here."

"Great. It's about time we had a mechanic in the family."

"But how did you break your hand?" Mike asked, watching the two men to see if they were about to pounce on him for taking the car last night. But they looked innocent. Dad wore his usual ancient white levis and a sweatshirt that looked as if it had been through the Civil War. Mom claimed he was opposed to wearing anything that hadn't hung in his closet at least ten years first. Seasoning, she called it. He looked as if he was dressed to help.

"How do you think I broke my hand?" Mr. Varian asked indignantly. "What would you have done to that fool donkey? Well, I leaned down to pick up a stick to give that dang animal the switching he so richly deserved and he stepped on my hand, if you really want to know."

"That's the story of my life," Mike said, and thought it was too bad he couldn't tell Mr. V. the story of the coyotes at Barbecue Flat and how the generator conked out when they needed it most. He might chance it if Dad weren't there. Anyone who found a donkey in heat when he was searching for gold just might understand.

"So just never count on there being safety in ignorance," the prospector said, turning the old generator over and looking at it carefully. "Mike, I think you ought to be able to trade this old generator in, all right. Probably make you four or five bucks. It was pretty near gone, though. See here where the brushes are all worn and the commutator's ground down. Bearings are loose and noisy too. Wonder this old wreck charged the battery at all—God must be kind to old men and young boys. This here generator has been in over forty thousand miles and with the night driving I did in Death Valley and your extra beacon light that's a good life. Mike, did you buy the ignition repair kit I mentioned?" he asked, putting the old generator off to one side regretfully, as if he were fond of the old part and hated to put it out to pasture.

"They were out of the kits so I got new points and a condenser. Dad thought that might be enough."

"Since the only other part normally in the kit is the rotor, and I've never had trouble with that gadget, what you got should fill the bill. Too bad, though, that you couldn't afford new plugs. They really make a difference."

"Can't squeeze blood from a turnip. Isn't that right, Mike?" Dad said. "Want to hand the plugs over, and I'll clean them up."

"This turnip is so dry you can't even get turnip juice," Mike said grimly, looking up as he worked on the distributor, putting in the points and adjusting them.

It was pleasant work. Dad and Peter Varian discussed the peculiarities of the buggy with fondness and the objectivity of surgeons, and Mike was surprised at his father's easy familiarity with the insides of a car. He had thought his insistence that Mike learn about engines had been a do-as-I-say-not-as-I-do infliction of father knows best. Apparently not!

Mike looked up from the car for a breath of fresh air and glanced through the lupines and eucalyptus and sand to the ocean. The ocean was a deep blue, Caribbean blue. Mr. Melgrove said this stretch of the Pacific took on the color and mood of the seven seas over the period of a year. He said it was the gray of the Atlantic during winter storms, like the Caribbean on a day like this, and Mexican Gulf green on a clear summer day. Not that there were *many* clear summer days. Almost every morning, at least, was foggy. Mike looked back to the eucalyptus tree and wondered again where the butterflies went in the winter and where Mary was right then. He should be finished soon, so he could go pick her up. Was he going to take a razzing about that key! Would it be a good idea to ask Dad to go along with him and Peter Varian to try out the car and pick up Mary? Maybe if he suggested that *Peter* drive because he knew the car best, Dad wouldn't explode about his son's lousy driving? It had been such a good day—so far. Maybe *Dad* would like to drive? Hey, now *that* was thinking! Mike was about to suggest it when Peter spoke.

"By the way, I was talking to your number one son over at his job the other day. Pat seemed a mite worried about his draft number coming up. Wanted to know if I knew anything about conscientious objectors, had any prejudice against them, if you had to have a strong church affiliation, etc. I didn't get the impression he'd been doing any research, more that it was an idea he was trying on for size. I had to admit I'd never given the matter much thought but I supposed that what I thought about a conscientious objector depended on what I'd thought of him before he got the new title."

"Did he ask you about running off to Canada and giving up his citizenship?" Mr. Lamon asked tensely.

Mike noticed that Dad's hand shook as he lit a cigarette.

"Yes, he said running off didn't seem to be working out too well from what he could see by the newspapers."

"Well, thank the Lord for that. His mother's been planting around every newspaper article she could find about guys who came home again. Maybe it took. He was Gung ho for Canada a couple of weeks ago. It's just damn hard to know—"

"Excuse me just a minute, sir? Now, Mike, just lay those screws on the fender there. I usually bring out a tarpaulin so I'll be sure to find everything, but they should be O.K. there. Mr. Lamon, I don't mind telling you I didn't know what to advise your boy. Fortunately he just seemed to need an ear—and, God knows, he's got my sympathy," the old prospector said, shaking his head.

"I don't *know* what to advise him, myself. His problems are big ones, and there's no telling him they'll go away in this best of all possible worlds. It certainly makes an adult of him in a hurry, because he'll have to serve out his decision, whatever it is.

"Mike doesn't know this yet, but Pat's lost his student deferment. He didn't want Mike to know because he thought maybe he could get the deferment back before Mike would have to know and be ashamed of him. Well, it didn't work. You have to stay in the top third of your class. He tried, but he's always had trouble with math and it finally sunk him. Pat says he's not afraid of dying, but he hates to become a cripple for a war he doesn't understand. On the other hand, this is his country and he doesn't want to break the law, either. His mother is hysterical, of course, and I don't mind telling you there are days when I feel pretty hysterical about the whole mess, myself."

Mike watched his father sit down in the velvet chair. Why, he was an old man, a tired old man. He sagged, and he was even losing his hair. And Mom had certainly looked like a before ad for the last couple of weeks. No wonder! He had known Pat was worried, but not to the extent of draft dodging. But then, how *would* he know since nobody in his own

133

family ever told him anything? Pat could come over and talk to Peter Varian, but he gave his kid brother driving lessons an hour a day without saying a single God-damned word.

That wasn't quite true. Pat had a whole series of war phrases he kept trotting out, and Mike had never bitten on any of them. Draftees were the disenfranchised fodder, victims of taxation without representation, students were the great emasculated American males who couldn't make a decision . . . that bit about making a decision seemed to be bugging him the most. Mike knew he hadn't pressed for more information because of some crazy fear of his own, so there was no point in blaming the family. And what would he have said if he *had* known?

Yeah, that was the point. How now, brown cow? Well, Pat for sure was not cut out for playing it noble and going to prison and somehow he didn't seem to belong emptying bedpans in some Army hospital for two years either. Not that he didn't have the guts, just not the persistance. It would be like swimming out to rescue him and then going down for the third time. Besides, Pat hadn't been to church in five years. He'd never make it. Damn it, this mess wasn't Pat's fault. Why did he have to *do* anything?

"Pat's always been a live-for-today kind of guy. I envied him, to tell the truth," Dad said with a sad shrug. "And now—"

"Well, he's not a basket case yet!" Mike exploded.

134

"I'm sorry. I mean, maybe he'll get drafted and spend the two years in Georgia or someplace. He's always been lucky."

"That's true," Peter Varian said, as he finished cleaning the spark plugs. Mike knew he should help, but he couldn't seem to move.

"Those damn grades don't mean a thing, not a thing," Mike yelled.

"Take it easy. Here, Mike, clean these," Peter said, handing him the plugs.

"Pat didn't want you to know about losing the deferment. He's afraid you'd think he was stupid."

"Oh, God. Who does he think he is? Everybody loves Pat—I mean, I always wanted to be him. Does he have to do everything better than me, too, all the time? I mean, he makes his decisions, and when I have to, let me make mine." He almost blurted out that Pat would never have stolen a key but stopped just in the nick of time. That would be all Dad needed. Ten new lines would appear on his face.

"You're quite right, Mike, and I suspect you'll do at least as well as any of us with your own decisions," his father said.

Mike stared. If only he had a tape recorder. Dad thought he'd do at least as well with his own decisions as any of them. That was news. He even sounded as if he meant it. That wasn't what he said during the driving lesson. Maybe he'd been worried about Pat that day.

135

"Dad, I just thought, couldn't Pat go in the medics? He's always had a yen for psychology, and he knows something about first aid; he could at least be doing something useful, something that seemed worthwhile."

"But he'd have to volunteer, and if he does that he has to sign up for three years. It's a long time, three years, and there's no guarantee you get what you ask for." Dad seemed to be talking to himself except that he kept looking straight at Mike, as if he was begging someone to come up with an answer. And when he hauled himself up out of Mr. Varian's chair, it was as if it took every last bit of energy he had, as if he needed a derrick.

Without thinking, Mike said, "Dad, did you know about Pat's deferment when we had the driving lesson?" He wanted to kick himself as soon as the words were out. Talk about saying the worst thing possible!

"You mean, was that why I was so bitchy that stormy day? Yes, I knew, but also I was worried as hell about your competitive driving. And I spent the next twenty-four hours arguing myself out of taking away your permit for six months until you came to your senses. That's how close a call you had. But Pat says you've calmed down, and I'm ready for another demonstration—anytime."

They faced each other. Did Dad think he was a heel for changing the subject away from Pat and his Army problems? But he felt suddenly close to Dad and felt he had wanted him to understand that terrible morning.

"I would like to go out with you again, sometime, when you feel up to it," Dad repeated gently.

"Sure, we'll test the generator. Let's go along the beach," Mike answered, smiling.

"You *may*, providing we ever get her in," Peter Varian replied caustically. "Mike, now where in tarnation did you put those screws?"

"On top of the fender like you said."

"Well, they are not there now." Peter Varian and Mike looked in the sand under the fender and found all but two of the screws. With a shrug the prospector took two screws from the old generator and helped Mike secure them all.

"Do as I say not as I do and always put a tarp down before you start fooling around with screws," he growled.

"O.K., let's go for that ride you promised me," Dad urged.

"Before we wash up or after," Mike asked, holding out his greasy hands.

"Worst thing in the world you can do is hurry a mechanic," Peter Varian groaned, holding up a screw that went somewhere and had better be put there before something fell out some day. Mike realized he didn't like being hurried. Still, Dad was anxious to go for a ride, to do something to take his mind off Pat and the draft.

He thought of the key in the sandbag and wished he could get rid of it. Sooner or later, he'd be tempted to use it again, and then it would be better not to have it around. But then there'd be nothing in resisting temptation, either.

Mike hesitated and finally, with a quick movement, he shoved the sandbag under the seat. Surely it would be safe there?

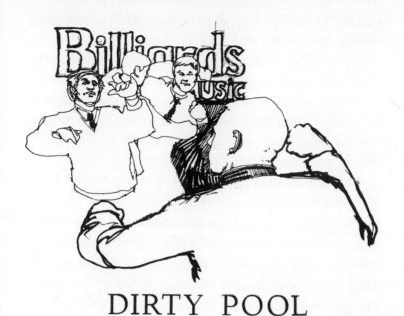

DIRTY POOL

BOTH THE stolen key and the sandbag disappeared from the car soon after New Year's. Mike and Pat went gaffing for steelhead one night with several friends and Mike never saw the sandbag again. Maybe it fell out of the car and into the creek? Or maybe someone picked it up and found the key when he dumped the sand? Or someone could have stolen the bag from the car and kept the key? He thought of changing the ignition but couldn't because then he'd have to explain what key he had lost. So he left it alone, knowing that if someone had the key he was free to come and claim the car whenever the spirit moved him. Since the Grasshopper had to be parked outside, it was easy pickings.

For a while Mike went home from school every afternoon expecting the car to be gone. However, when one month and finally two months went by and the dune buggy still sat in the driveway, the missing key blended with everything else that was going wrong and Mike almost forgot about it.

This was partly because he hardly ever got to drive. Nobody did because it rained so much that the only pleasure left was checking new inches-of-rainfall records. One storm followed another, pelting them with rain day after day until each house was like an ark. Main street was flooded for over a month, and only the sandbags piled eight deep along both sides saved the stores. As usual during bad winters, people listened to the raging rampaging ocean and worried about shipwrecks and tidal waves.

But at least Mike and his father did get out to school every morning. Anything was better than sitting at home listening to the rain and watching Pat and Mom wait for the mail, waiting to see if Uncle Sam had sent his greeting. Pat had dropped geometry so he didn't have any morning classes, and the two of them were like zombies until they heard the letters drop through the slot and hit the floor. Then Pat sat absolutely still until Mom rushed over, picked up the mail, and let out her soap opera sigh. Nothing. That meant Pat might as well go on to his afternoon classes. Sometimes he'd done his homework and sometimes he hadn't. He said he wanted to pass but there didn't seem to be much point in breaking his neck for grades anymore.

At the end of February Mary came down with mononucleosis. Mike took a constant ribbing about her getting the "kissing" disease; and he found when he phoned her that all she wanted to talk about were her symptoms. He tried to remind her of hunting for arrowheads and getting chased by coyotes, but she only wondered if she'd gotten the first chill then. He mentioned the dune buggy, and she warned him not to go out in the cold. It was too bad she was sick, but she didn't have to make such a production of it, did she?

It seemed a long time until there was any reason for celebrating anything, or any way of doing it. But finally it hadn't rained in a week, Mary was back on deck, and Mike wanted to get out. Pat and Annie said they'd double with them on Saturday night. So they had transportation and company. And they decided to go to the new pool hall, the first teen-age nightclub within fifty miles.

Saturday morning it was dry enough for Mike and Pat to earn their date money picking winter peas. The pay was good if you remembered to look under the vines. And it was good to get out in the fields under a clear sky and smell the peas and the earth itself, still steaming after the rains. It was like escaping from jail to stand in the center of twenty acres of peas and look back to the mesa and the foothills and up to the sky, and then turn and find the town and the glistening white sands and the ocean beyond.

"Man, this is living!" Mike said.

"Man, you are the living end is what you mean." Pat laughed. "Here I am—fingers raw to the bone from snapping off these damn peas that no one but a vegetarian wants anyhow, soaked through and blasted by wind and wet sand and *you're* living! My only consolation is that I probably won't come down with pneumonia until *after* our date tonight."

"You'd rather be smog-bound in Los Angeles?"

"If I were warm and dry, yes. But I'd really rather be in a gas station tonight with you filling up the tank on my Corvair." Pat grinned.

"All right. All right. I said I'd pay and I will, but it's extortion. Just two more months, and I'll have my own license."

"Blackmail," Pat said, grinning. "But don't forget that your popcorn machine takes gas, too."

"Yeah, but *I* don't mind working!"

"Wait until you find something better to do, sucker," Pat said grimly.

By that night it had turned cold and there was the feeling of another storm in the air. Wild and raw and alive. Mary and Annie were bundled in coats, scarves, boots.

"We'll never get to you," Pat complained.

"Chastity belts," Annie replied calmly.

Mike could feel Mary's hand stiffen in his. He wanted to tell her that this was just Annie's way of talking and meant nothing. This could turn out to be one long painful evening if Mary went into an injured virtue act like Mom sometimes did about Annie. Personally, he'd always liked Annie. She had been Pat's girl for three years, and as far as he could see Pat was damn lucky to have someone who understood him, was almost always good-natured, and who looked like Miss America.

Maybe this double dating was a bad idea. Maybe Pat and Annie were too slick for them. Mary hadn't said one word since she climbed in the Corvair. She *could* be waiting for him to break the silence. But nothing he could think to say sounded right for everyone. He could kid with Pat and Annie, but then Mary wouldn't be in on the joke. He could talk with Mary, make contact again, but that was apt to sound like sweet fifteen to Pat in the front seat. Fortunately, they'd be at the pool hall in minutes, and Mary was an absolute demon about games. She should like that, anyhow.

"Mike, have you ever played pool before?" Mary whispered.

He nodded sadly. "Don't worry, I'll teach you. It's easy," he whispered back. Lord, Pat and Annie were regular pool sharks. No wonder Mary was quiet. Why hadn't she said she didn't play pool when he'd told

143

her about the new pool hall? He had played with Pat and Annie at the college. Oh, well, too late to worry now. Here goes nothing, Mike thought, as Pat swung the Corvair into the parking lot alongside the brightly lighted billiard parlor.

"Looks just like the old saloons in all the TV movies about San Francisco," Pat said.

And it did. A gold canopy hung over the sidewalk for the length of the building. "The Joynt" was written in bare electric bulbs above the canopy. They pushed open the heavy carved wooden doors to find they were in a Victorian gambling hall. The floors were covered with plush red carpeting. One wall was lined with psychedelic posters and another with what looked like original oil paintings of the ocean and sand dunes. The walls themselves were of dark wood and on them were mounted rose glass tear drop lamps, which appeared to provide the only light. How did anyone see to play pool?

"Like wow!" Annie said.

"Amen!" Mary laughed.

"Care to take a number and sit down while you're waiting? Our tables are full just now. There's a coke bar if you want anything to eat or drink," a young man in a gay nineties straw hat, striped vest, and arm bands told them.

"It's like a palace—" Mary whispered. "It's the most wonderful place I've ever been in my whole life."

"It's comfortable—like a bar. I've always wanted to

be twenty-one so I could go in a bar and just sit. Look, they're dancing—" Annie added.

"Sure, we'll take a number," Pat said happily.

"How did you know? I didn't even know it was here," Mike asked as he threaded his way through the cue sticks and players to the soft drink bar. Comfortable chairs and sofas were grouped around a fireplace beyond a small raised dance floor where couples danced to an organ playing rock.

"I just found out it was opening last week."

"Well, they sure didn't advertise." Apparently they didn't need to. "The Joynt" was crowded.

"Dancing in stocking feet only," Mary read and kicked off her boots and started rocking in time to the music.

"Now you're back. Hello," Mike rocked with her, jerking his body and his head in time to some private direction the music had only for him and Mary.

"Nice to see you again," he yelled.

"Like coming alive," Mary replied.

Mike nodded. She *was* coming alive. The color was coming to her cheeks, the joy to her smile, and the tenderness and wildness to her eyes. He reached out for one hand and swung her high and wide, close and far out and reaching her close again, caught in the music and hardly aware of his own steps. Aware only when the music stopped for a moment of a kaleidoscopic blur of Annie and Pat, the reds and blues of other people, the slam of billiard balls and the intrusion of other voices.

He was sorry when their table came up. He put one hand lightly against Mary's cheek. "May I have the first dance after the game?" he whispered.

"Come on! Did we come to play pool? Hurry up or we'll lose our turn," Pat yelled from their table where he was rubbing the cues with chalk, critically checking each one to make sure the blue chalk covered the end before laying it aside and taking up another.

"All right, we're coming. Relax."

"Just can't wait to make the kill, Pat?" Mary called as they wove through the tables toward their own, on the far side of the room.

"Yeah, you were probably born under a pool table! Your grandfather says the only reason he's teaching you chess is that you beat him at all the games you already know. Don't kid me with that innocent bit, Mary," Pat said as Mary picked up a stick and threatened to hit him over the head with it.

"Numbers or scramble?" Annie asked, obviously anxious to get started. She was a good player, and Mike knew she was looking forward to a good game from Mary after Pat's buildup. Poor Mary. If only he'd had a chance to coach her a little.

"Depends on the wager," Pat suggested, raising an eyebrow.

"No bets. This is the first time I've ever played," Mary said.

"The hell it is! You handle that stick like a pro."

"Scramble. Give her the benefit of the doubt for one game at least," Annie decided. "Mary and I will take on you and Mike."

Mike started to protest. Then his face tightened. He looked at Mary and then significantly toward the door. A group of young men stood just inside, gathered around a huge Marine in full dress uniform.

Mary whistled softly.

"Look who's joined the Marines," Pat said. There was something in his voice that bothered Mike. Something like admiration.

"He's still Trouble in my book," Annie growled.

"Amen," Mary added.

"He just had to have a uniform, didn't he? And when he couldn't get into college and a football jersey, he took what he could get. Come on, let's play pool," Annie said, turning her back on the crowd gathering around Trouble. "Who breaks?"

Mike thought Trouble looked even bigger in the smart blue dress uniform, and unusually clean and well-dressed in the midst of levis and plaid wool shirts. His voice, always gravelly and loud, now seemed to dominate the room. His was the only voice you could hear above the rock music of the organ and the slam-wham of pool balls. They couldn't help hearing what he'd told the examining doctors, the preferential treatment he got for volunteering, or what he'd do to the cowardly enemy.

"Me, I just see *myself* jumping around from bush to

bush out in those jungles—bouncing, dodging, hiding—" Pat mumbled.

"Yeah? That's cause you can see, and he's just pretending he's on T.V.," Annie said, giving the white ball a vicious jab that slammed three balls into pockets.

"Wow! Hurray! Now beat that." Her second shot netted her nothing.

"Well, don't get greedy."

"Hey, what have we over here. Who's celebrating?" Trouble peered through the darkness. No one said anything. Mike and Mary took their shots in silence.

"Can't see through this damn darkness," Trouble said as he started toward them. He stumbled, swore, and lurched from table to table, disrupting games, but still coming straight for them.

"He's been hitting the bottle," Pat whispered. "Hi, Trouble. Congratulations, man," he said aloud.

"Well, old Pat hasn't made the grade yet. Still dodging the draft? No offense, Pat, put her there," Trouble said, sticking out his hand.

Pat took it. His face was set.

"And Little Miss Mary, quite contrary. Still playing the minor leagues, I see."

"I'm satisfied," Mary said and turned to watch Annie shoot.

"Well, suppose *I'm* not?" Trouble reached toward Mary, but it was dark and he was unsteady and Pat intercepted him and shook hands again.

"So you went ahead and did it—signed up, the full route. Remember the last time I saw you? We were both trying to decide," Pat said.

"Yeah. Flim-flam-damn. I got to thinking. My country needs me—hell—it's a lead pipe cinch no one else does. Commies—here's lead in your guts. Ain't no one gonna say *I'm* yellow."

Trouble looked around him belligerently. Someone patted him on the back and he relaxed. Annie pulled at Pat to make his shot. Pat missed the ten ball. Trouble chuckled.

Mike opened his mouth to tell the tall Marine off but thought better of it. Why cause a fuss? If they ignored him, something else would prove more interesting and he'd go away. That was Trouble's bag— excitement and glory. There were no touchdowns at this table, and when he realized it, he'd move on. Mike watched Mary take her shot from across the table even though it would be better from this side. She didn't want to risk getting within grabbing distance, and he didn't blame her. Talk about the long arm of the Marines.

"Not very sociable—considering—"

"Well, it takes a good man to be able to make up his mind, I'll say that for you, Trouble." Pat broke the silence, and his voice was unsteady, upset.

"Damn right. I was a good man on the team, too. Right, Sophomore wonder!"

Mike nodded and tried to grin. He'd never liked

149

Trouble calling him the Sophomore wonder, but Trouble never lost the opportunity to bring it up. Maybe Pat was just the fall guy because Mike got on the team so young. Or maybe Trouble just wanted every ounce of glory he figured was coming and making Pat look bad made him look better.

It wasn't like Trouble to drop needling if he saw it was working, and any fool could see he'd gotten to Pat. How far could they let him carry it? Mike had never had a real fight and he wondered if Pat had. If he had, he'd sure kept it a deep dark secret. Trouble and his pals, on the other hand, wore their knuckles bare every weekend. To say nothing of being eighty pounds heavier. And how about hitting a man in uniform? Was it against the law? And how about the "Joynt?" Wouldn't do much for a new place to have problems right off the bat.

Mike looked around. Annie was racking up the balls for another game. Mary concentrated on chalking the sticks, keeping her eyes down on the table. Pat said something to Trouble, something that caught him off guard.

Why didn't he take off? All around them people were laughing and relaxed, having the good time they'd had until this self-styled hero showed up. The low lights, the sounds of balls, the dancing and tinkle of glasses in the background all made Mike feel like an outsider. No, Trouble was the outsider. He was ruining it all, ruining their good evening.

"You don't see what I'm getting at, Trouble. Take that chip off your shoulder—just for a minute—man. I'm admiring you not attacking you. All I want to know is, how did you decide? You know, volunteering means three years of your life and maybe the last three. I mean, what makes it worth the basket case risk?"

Trouble hesitated. He was pale, and as he leaned on the pool table Mike saw that his hand shook.

"Look, Rum-dum, maybe—maybe—it doesn't take a congressional investigation. Like they say, the human body is worth less than a dollar. So why sweat it? Besides, God knows there's nothing to do around this lousy town. Talk about dull. Man, you'll have to admit I'm right on the nail there. So, I aim to be where the action is. Think about it that way, Pat!" There was a strident plaintive quality in Trouble's voice that made them all, even the players from the next table, stop and stare at him. Trouble shifted from one foot to the other and shrugged.

"He sounds trapped," Mary whispered.

"What's that, Mary always contrary? If you got anything to say about Trouble, let's hear it loud and clear, right, boys?"

Trouble's friends nodded without enthusiasm.

"Let's shove off. I need a drink," someone said.

"I'm waiting, babe," Trouble repeated.

"Pick on somebody your own size," Annie suggested.

"I said that you sounded as if you were trapped," Mary repeated clearly.

"What do you mean, trapped?"

"Like maybe you felt down one day and went out and joined the Marines," Mary said.

So it was out, Mike thought. Kind of rough on Trouble, but someone had to say it for Pat.

Trouble's little blue eyes narrowed so that they were almost hidden in the fold between his jutting cheek bones and his overhanging brows. Mike had seen the same look on his face just before he tackled some guy who'd cleated him on the football field. The team called it Trouble's hell-for-leather look.

"We done, gang? The girls won. Let's take off," Mike said abruptly, picking up Mary's coat and his own jacket. Annie needed no urging.

Trouble snatched the coat and jacket so fast that Mike hardly knew they were gone. Trouble handed them on to one friend, who in turn passed them on to someone else. Trouble still had said nothing. Now he moved slowly over to the other side of the table where he faced Mary directly.

"You skirts can say any damn thing you want, and we still have to go out and rot in the jungles just so you *can* sound off. And if I don't come back, just you remember what you said tonight!"

"I didn't start the conversation or choose the subject," Mary said quietly, firmly.

"Who are you calling names?" Mike asked, moving up to challenge the big Marine. He was deftly intercepted by one of the smiling attendants in the striped shirts and straw hats. At the same time the organ played *The Marines Hymn*. Trouble smiled.

"Hey, that's my song."

"That's right, Private. And we have a table for you now, if you'd like."

Trouble looked over to the three boys with him and they nodded. He hesitated, eyeing Mary again. Everyone was silent, and the sound of rain beating steadily on a tin roof contrasted sharply with the plush opulence of the rugs and the soft lighting. "The Joynt" was still a warehouse, after all, just a warehouse with rugs.

One of Trouble's friends handed Mike the coat and jacket, then put one arm around Trouble's shoulder and nodded. They'd take Trouble away. Mary was pulling at his other sleeve. What was he supposed to do? Let that bully say anything he pleased to Mary and walk out scot free? But Trouble *was* in uniform, and if Mary was right, he must feel pretty low. All right. Mike shrugged and turned back to their table. He took up his cue. It was his turn, anyhow. They could at least finish the game.

Trouble looked around to see who was watching. Mary had moved to the other side of the table. His friends were calling from their table across the room. Everyone else was playing pool. He shrugged and turned to follow the attendant in the candy striped shirt. Suddenly, without warning, he whipped around and lunged for Mike's pool stick.

"Ugh! He jabbed me! He deliberately poked me. My back was turned and the bastard went after me! Shot me in the back," Trouble bellowed.

"Then how come you're holding your stomach?" Annie laughed.

Maybe it was the laugh that finally did it. Maybe Trouble just didn't like being told what to do. At any rate he started swinging then, wildly, just as if he had to swing. When he caught Mike on the jaw, he wasn't in close enough for it to do much damage. Mike stepped back and saw Trouble land a right in Pat's stomach. Pat dodged behind the table.

Before Mike could circle around, the big tackle had dumped over the table, pelting them with balls. Dimly he heard people screaming and maybe other people fighting. He peered through the dark for the big Marine and got another sock on the jaw, this one connecting in a flash of lights and searing pain. All right, if that was the way he wanted to play Mike could dish it out too. He found himself hitting wildly, aiming for the big Marine's stomach, pummeling him now, feeling nothing. Then he found himself face to face with Trouble, the ugly pig eyes pressed right against his own. Mike couldn't believe what he saw. Trouble's eyes were happy. Happy! There was no fury or hatred but a kind of joy and something else. Trouble was figuring the odds, just like on the field.

Mike stopped dead. His hands dropped.

Trouble belted him one on the jaw. As he went down, Mike saw Pat move in over him and thrusting forward like a snake deliver a series of quick jabs at the face looking down at him. It was like watching a movie. He saw blood spurt and wondered if it would fall on him.

The next thing Mike knew they were out on the sidewalk, the concrete hard against his back and the rain pelting him in the face. So it was raining again. Someone had raised his head. Mary. It was uncomfortable. He had an awful headache.

"Mary? Is it all over?"

"Pat, he's come to. How do you feel, Mike?"

"Trouble wasn't mad. It was just another football game. Where is he?"

"Taken off. And we'd better follow or the police will have themselves some fall guys," Pat said, holding an ice pack to his jaw. Where did he get the ice? Must be cold in the rain.

It was strange lying on the sidewalk under the electric bulbs flashing "The Joynt" on and off, on and off. Had that been Trouble's blood dropping on him? Must not have been too bad if he'd gone. Never mind. He didn't want to move. Pat and Mary and Annie wanted him to, but he felt dizzy when his head was lifted. The rain was surprisingly warm. Like a lukewarm shower that went on and on after the thirty-gallon tank ran dry. Maybe everyone else should cut out and he'd just roll over into a shadow where no one would notice him.

"Are you all O.K.?"

"You were the only casualty," Pat said. "Trouble said to tell you that you could fight on his side, anytime."

"I was nasty to him," Mary said, and there were tears in her eyes. Or maybe it was the rain.

"Rain feels sooo good," Mike said.

"Look, we've got to get out of here. You take his feet and I'll take his head," Annie said.

"My head hurts," Mike announced.

"Just let me drag him to the car," Pat said.

Mike sat up. They were serious. He could almost feel his head bumping all the way around to the parking lot. The parking lot was mud.

"I'm getting up. Did we wreck "The Joynt?""

"Pushed over the table is all. Those attendants must be trained in judo and riot tactics both. They had us out of there and the table in use again before most people knew what had happened."

"Or cared," Mike groaned.

"One thing I'll say for you. A date with you isn't dull," Mary said as she led Mike to the car.

SMASH UP

MIKE TOOK a deep breath. He absorbed the bite of salt
and the heavy sweet verbena and the whipping sandy
wind and he let up on the accelerator a little. Not that
he felt better, nothing could help that much, but tearing down the beach in a breakneck competition with
the tide did make it all bearable.

How many times before had he come to the beach
when a great day had gone bust? How many other
birthdays had he muffed? Birthdays had always been
prone to disaster, and he should have known better
than to take his driving test on one. Last year, for ex-

ample, he'd had the worst fight of his life with Dad, and on his thirteenth birthday he'd gotten a concussion when his surfboard hit a submerged rock. And at ten his party had been the absolute flop of the year. Half the kids hadn't even come. From now on he would not even get out of bed on any birthday!

But, even so, who could have predicted that he'd be stupid enough to run Pat's Corvair up over the curb trying to park? Not many people had that much talent for self-destruction, especially when they had passed a driving test. The inspector had even stopped jerking to attention at every stop and turn. The great stone face had already marked the test. Parking was almost an afterthought, and he'd swung into the roped off area with relief. That was the trouble. Never relax. You just *don't* flip a wheel with power steering the way you do a stiff wheel like the one on the Grasshopper. One little flip, and there they were with the Corvair's hind end upon the curb.

As the examiner said, "Good God."

"Well, here's sand in your eyes, Pat," Mike yelled over the pounding of the ocean and the engine. There was no reason to shout because Pat sat right beside him, hunched into a ball against the stinging wind; but the echo of the sound left a satisfying tingle all the way down his throat.

"Fog's closing in. Funny. It's supposed to lift about noon," Pat complained.

"You have to admit, this has been a backward day

all around." Mike laughed and it sounded hollow and bitter, ugly. He'd better shut up if he couldn't do better than that.

The foghorn sounded offshore, somehow solidifying the fogbank drifting in. Already the wind was dragging the first gray wisps around and past them on into the yellow dunes. And beyond the dunes the town and the mountains were splotchy, unreal, one moment crystal clear and the next obscured with a barely discernible haze. It was as if you were being fitted for glasses and they kept changing the lenses in that black box, Mike thought. It wouldn't be long now. Between the rising tide and the rain-swollen creek and the fog closing in, he didn't have much time.

A sea gull dropped a clam. The cracked shell lay a hundred feet or so ahead in the rubble of shells ground up in breakers and seaweed left from a past high tide. Mike had plenty of time to swerve but instead he speeded up and savagely smashed the clam while the swooping gull scurried for its life, squawking furiously.

"You won. He'll never come back for that clam!" Pat chuckled uneasily.

"His tough luck then. I was only trying to help him crack the damn clam was all. Some days you can't even treat a gull right."

He didn't usually go in for terrorizing birds or ruining their meals, but this wasn't a day for picking on somebody your own size. He pressed the accelerator all the way to the floor. It was a good beach for a run. The sand was still packed hard from the late April rains, but it had a spring, a buoyancy, that gave some traction.

"Mike! Take it easy, man. Look, high tide and low fog mean dune rider beware. Maybe we'd better head for the pier and—"

"And go home and cut the birthday cake?" Even Mike was shocked by the bitterness in his voice. Better get hold of himself. "Just give me another twenty minutes here on the beach, Pat? Please. I need to unwind. Then we'll head straight home and face the music. O.K.?"

"Sure, no sweat. Must have almost an hour before the tide gets too high to cross the creek. But, look, Mike, don't make a federal case out of flunking one miserable little driving test. You got a bitch of an examiner and we guessed wrong in having you take the test with the Corvair instead of your popcorn machine. But that is *all*. You must have had ninety percent until the parking. Another two weeks and you can take it again."

"And again and again and again? Don't blame it on him. Don't do that, Pat! He didn't back your Corvair up over a foot high curb, did he? Well, did he? No, indeed. And just wait until that great Driver Ed. instructor, the prophet of the marble orchard, hears. And you can bet Dad will tell him," Mike said fiercely.

"Down, boy. So the examiner's a father image. That's O.K. with me. Just forget this big drama about going home to face the music is all. If you think anyone except you is going to think anything more than too bad you won't have your license for another two weeks, you are mistaken. If you'd flunked all the exams I have in nineteen years, you'd understand that. Mom and Dad are well broken in. Nobody else gives a damn, except the draft board, of course." Pat shrugged and let his voice trail off.

Mike knew he was thinking about his losing his student deferment, the blow-up with Trouble at the pool hall, and maybe there was already a notice from the draft board lying in his top middle bureau drawer at home. Pat acted as if he were about to be detonated. Pow! So Pat had bigger troubles than he did. So what?

One day he'd graduate to that nightmare, too. Manhood. Always a bigger misery tomorrow unless you stepped on a grenade today. Then it was all over—if you were lucky, if not you ended up spending the next forty years in a wheelchair or a basket. But meanwhile, today was supposed to be one of those landmarks, his sixteenth birthday. It even started out with champagne. Pat had put the bottle, packed in ice, and two glasses on the table by Mike's alarm clock so he'd see it when he woke up. Maybe they should have drunk the champagne instead of trotting off to the Motor Vehicle Department. But he had wanted to celebrate by getting his driver's license first thing.

"Afraid you'll have to come back and see us in two weeks, young man, and you'll do us all a favor if you practice before you try again," the examiner had said instead of issuing the license. At least he hadn't added all that bit about safe driving and the life you save may be your own. Maybe enough sixteen-year-olds had hauled off and socked enough examiners so they had cut the sermon. But the point was clear. Flunk out.

Mike traced the path of the tide, pushing his foot down hard on the accelerator, skidding the car through the rising breakers. They didn't have much time. They couldn't stay on the beach much longer. So they'd better make full use of it while they could. There had been other bad days when he'd just sat in the warm hollow of a dune until all the bitterness had drained and he had gradually absorbed a lonely sort of peace.

But today he wanted to take on the wind and the fog, to bite the salt spray, to give the Grasshopper a run for her life on the hard packed beach and to challenge the arrogant May ocean. He wanted to be free for half an hour.

"No one's on the beach that I can see, Pat. O.K. if I open her up?"

Pat grinned and nodded. He pulled a knitted cap over his ears and snapped on the seat belt. "Let her rip, man. Not even the tourists are dumb enough to be out clamming with a plus two tide *and* fog coming in."

Nevertheless, Mike took the buggy another ten feet

up from the tide line. He'd hate to reach eighty for the first time and suddenly see a couple of figures hunched over clamming forks looming out of the fog. There were lots of madmen in this world. He shifted his weight, pulled down his jacket, crouched over the wheel and let out the throttle. For years he'd looked forward to making a run. Look out sea gulls! Look out pelicans!

"The gulls better believe we can fly too," he shouted joyously. His foot held the accelerator to the floor. He caught one last look at Pat's face and was surprised at the intensity of delight and fear. Pat *really* dug this racing bit. He must want to be driving now if he felt so powerfully! Generous guy, that big brother. Then he turned full attention to the driving. The speedometer hit sixty as he swerved to miss a driftwood log, and kept inching its way up, flickering at seventy. Holding, holding, and then finally slowly reaching for the seventy-five mark. Maybe seventy-five was top speed for this turtle on wheels.

They were doing seventy-five when they started across the creek bed, hit a clump of seaweed, jumped high over the rest of the creek and landed on all fours on the opposite bank. God, that was close. Didn't want to go that route again. Mike slowed to sixty and held it there over the clear beach. What else was ahead? He tried to remember. Nothing permanent. No old car hulks or decaying sea lions or washed up telephone poles along here. Nothing, then. The tide had not been high since he'd last walked the beach. He'd have to watch it down by the big dunes beyond Barbecue Flats, though, but that was a mile yet.

All right, then, he told the car. Make it to eighty, you old turtle on wheels, make it to eighty! The needle started climbing again. Seventy. Seventy-five. Who ever heard of a Volkswagen doing eighty? Who would ever believe she had it in her? Seventy-eight.

"Eighty miles an hour! Eighty miles an hour!" Mike screamed above the pulsing car. The fog was soupy here and so there was no outside. They could run right off the world.

"Ultimate!" Pat shouted back. And in his shout Mike heard a sigh of joy and release as clearly as he heard an unspoken command to slow down. It was over then? That was all? The car vibrated as if it would splinter into a million pieces. Mike knew *that* feeling, and he responded by taking his foot off the accelerator. He'd splintered too at the end of football workout sometimes when the coach urged him around the field once again until he felt his heart would burst.

But he did not feel anything now. He was going faster in the car than on the football field. That was all. Nothing. Empty. He didn't even feel fear, though he knew that came from enormous ignorance. Maybe the thrill took another minute or so to sink in, or maybe it didn't come the first time you hit eighty. Or maybe he was just square.

Mike eased off a little, down to seventy, down to

sixty-five. Pat slumped in the seat beside him, and a low satisfied whistle escaped him. At least Mike had shown Pat he could do it. That was some accomplishment, wasn't it?

The car contracted in a series of rattles and thumps and gradually quieted. Sixty was a good speed for the Grasshopper. The car sounded as if it were purring. Pat looked content too. Sixty? It felt as if they were doing twenty-five after the strain of eighty. Slow and easy. Eighty hadn't done a thing for him. Maybe because he wasn't doing anything but pressing the accelerator while the car rattled its guts? After bursting your own guts on the football field maybe pushing at something else just wasn't enough?

Smug thought. Well, whatever the deep psychological reasons, his first burst of speed had been great for Pat and had done nothing for him. Now, if they didn't get off the beach before the tide came in and the fog got so thick you couldn't tell where the ocean was, they could lose the buggy altogether. That was the strange thing about fog. You lost your sense of direction.

How far down were they? Two miles? Through the drifting fog, the dunes looked big. The big dunes only started beyond Barbecue Flats. They must have come at least three or four miles then. The ocean floor dropped off sharply that far down. No place to get caught in a riptide, or stuck, or marooned. Better turn the buggy around and head for the pier while he still had some idea where he was and still had some chance of avoiding driftwood.

Sand was loose. He'd have to turn toward the water or they might get stuck in the loose sand. Especially today because he'd forgotten to let air out of the tires. Damn. Lucky there weren't any clammers. There couldn't be. Nothing for it but to swing toward the breakers and the sooner the better. All right. Deep breath. Turn now.

"Hey, don't do that! Slow down to forty first. Slow down. Mike! Crazy fool. God damn it, you're out of your mind. Slow·down!"

At least he doesn't grab the wheel like Dad does, Mike thought. But what does he expect me to do? It's too late. Back up? Don't slow in the turn. You'll skid, Dad says. Can't skid. Land in the water. Oops, here we go, over on two wheels. Have to brake. Bucking bronco. Sorry. Have to.

"Pat. Ballast, ballast! God damn. Lean to the dunes. Ballast! Help me, help me. More. Good, now. It's bucking. No!"

Mike felt as if he was in a dream, fighting his way up through layers of water into the morning. Had the alarm gone off? He'd heard something. Must be time to get up. It was cold. And wet. Mike opened his eyes. He was in the ocean, the tide. Water seeped around him. His eyes stung from the salt. He lay on his back. Must sit up. What was that? A pelican? Your beak can hold more than your belly can. Ugly brown pelican looking for a fish. Must think he's a whale. Maybe thinks the whale will regurgitate some fish. Too bad, hungry brown pelican. Poor pelican, go away. That's right, be afraid, go away. Sit up. What happened? What was he doing out there. Must have wiped out again. But he hadn't been on a surfboard in months. No. Well. No, there'd been a car. But he wasn't in a car. He heard a motor running. Couldn't see a thing. Damn fog. Where, where was the sound coming from?

A wave engulfed him and he spun crazily, drowning, drowning after all. Never thought of going that way. And then, inexplicably, the water was gone and he was still alive, still breathing. Cold. Cold. Shivering. He was shivering and, therefore, he must be alive. He dug into the sand, clutching for a hold like a sand crab, inching his way as he'd seen a sand crab do. The sand crab, however, knew what direction it wanted to travel. Or didn't care.

He'd been in a car and he could still hear its motor, so maybe he should aim toward the sound. There was some other reason he should find the car, but he couldn't remember. Just now he couldn't remember. Got dizzy when he tried to remember. Never mind. The car was near. He'd reach the car and then think. If it weren't for the fog, he could see it. Near.

Again the water engulfed him, but this time he moved up and the water only swirled around his waist and then drew back again. He must hurry before it came again. It would come again and again. Crawl. No. With shoes he couldn't dig in like a crab. Take off the shoes. Then the socks. Better to get up on his knees and then the legs could help. Hurry. Crawl toward the engine. Good engine to keep going. Never mind the water because you never were going to drown. It was always Pat who was going to drown.

"Pat! Pat! The turn. Pat!" He'd been making a turn, and Pat was in the car. Pat always thought he was going to drown, even hated swimming. Pat sat on the beach with friends and seldom even played in the breakers. Pat swam out to save him and had to be rescued. It would be his fault if Pat drowned. He'd been driving and made a turn too fast. He killed—

"Pat!!!!!!!!" But Pat must have been thrown from the car, too. Maybe he was lying in the surf unconscious. "Pat, for God's sakes, answer me. Please! Don't die! Pat! I didn't mean to do it. I didn't mean to drown you. Please!"

He had to find Pat. He couldn't cry. No time. He must stand up. Good. He seemed to be whole. Arms and legs worked. He kept seeing Pat's face the day he had fallen off the surfboard and Pat had come to the rescue. His face had been drawn, white, stretched taut, and worst of all, accepting. There'd been no real danger. The undertow had pulled, but only downbeach, not further out. Here the undertow would take you straight out to sea. Had to find Pat.

"The green octopus. The green octopus has got me

at last," he had said. And above them the sun had shone and on the nearby beach the gang had talked and been completely unaware.

Mike knew he couldn't stand to see Pat like that again. Couldn't stand knowing it was his fault. Got to get to the car. Damn engine was sputtering. It might stop, even with a new generator it might stop in the ocean. Would stop. His sense of direction was shot by the fog and the ringing in his head, but the noise seemed to come from the left, from the water. Dear God, from the water! Hang on Pat. Hang on engine.

The engine sputtered feebly and stopped. The fog horn shattered the eerie silence, shattered the last hope of remembering the direction of that last feeble sputtering. The fog was like a white moonless night. He could hardly see his hand groping out in front of him. Still, he followed the way the hand had pointed when the fog horn disconnected him from the car sound.

And suddenly he remembered that Pat had had his seat belt on, was belted into the car, and was probably still pinioned to the front seat. He heard again the sharp metallic snap as clearly as when Pat put on the belt. So he was still in the car, probably crushed and waiting while the water crept closer and closer. While it washed out and came in again. He could drown knowing its full slow terror, every last horror. Then let him be dead already, killed instantly by a merciful concussion.

Mike was steadily probing the fog, stumbling over

great mounds of seaweed, a box, a beer can, even over soaking freezing feet that no longer seemed a part of his body. Methodically, unthinking, he stopped now and then to rub his legs and hands to return circulation when they got numb and caused him to stumble. He must not fall again.

And he kept calling Pat's name. It was so short the sound faded almost immediately. Patrick. Patrick. No. Pat's face seemed everywhere backed by a dream of white fog and the feel of that day Pat swam out to rescue him, fused with the more recent terror and joy on Pat's face on that wild ride before the accident. It *had* been an accident. The accident was caused by turning too fast. Pat and Dad both had said not to turn fast. Not to brake on a turn?

Finally—after hours or days or only minutes—he stumbled over a soft mound. Mike felt the body. Pat! Pat!

"Oh, no. No! Help!" Mike screamed as he saw Pat's face, the parchment skin, the gaping mouth, the lower part of the body disemboweled. Intestines spilling out. Oh, God no! No legs. Where were Pat's legs? And brown? Jacket? Pat had on the blue parka he'd given him for Christmas. Wait a minute. The stink? Pat couldn't smell of death already, could he? Terrible smell, and it was usually hard to smell anything lapped by salt water. Fur. Pat didn't have fur. Not Pat. Pat might be all right. Not Pat but a sea lion washed up on the beach and already decaying and his guts pouring out. Already a focus for flies even in the fog.

Mike stumbled on and saw a faint green tinge to a lump of the fog. And moving in on it he saw spinning wheels, sickening in their reminder of terror and an uncompleted turn, the wheels still turning in the air. But they were a relief compared to the memory of the sea lion. The Grasshopper lay overturned like some monstrous sick light, some futile beacon in the fog. Terrible in its silence.

"Pat?" Mike asked quietly.

Nothing. Mike hesitated to call again, unwilling to break the eerie quiet, to finally learn the truth. Pat could have been thrown clear. The seat belt could have broken. Dad hadn't bought the best. Or Pat could have unsnapped it in that final instant. He had enough presence of mind for that. But he could be under the car.

The foghorn shrieked. The water was rising still. Quickly Mike went to the car. He did not call again. He looked under the door and saw a dangling hand and a leg thrown out in an impossible angle and pinned under the back of the seat. He recognized the gray and maroon argyle socks Mom had knitted Pat for Christmas.

"Pat! Are you all right, alive. Please oh please, Pat, answer me. You haven't drowned, Pat, you haven't drowned. The water hasn't reached you yet. Pat!"

There was no answer. The feet lay still. The foghorn howled its mournful dirge, and all was silent.

SURVIVAL

THE SILENCE was terrible. Mike felt his own heart pounding in sickening contrast to the still legs protruding from under the overturned car. He was a blobby, vibrating jellyfish while Pat lay still. He called as much to hear some sound as because he hoped for an answer. There was no answer, and he was no longer surprised. After all, hadn't he called a dozen, half a hundred times and been slapped with the silence? The wind lashed his wet clothes against him, but still he stood looking at the accident.

Finally, he did what he had known he must do but

postponed because he was afraid. He bent down and felt for a pulse on the pinioned leg. The pulse thundered through his whole body. A strong regular pulse. But perhaps he'd gotten his own. Methodically, he tried again, being careful not to test with his index finger. No, it was Pat's pulse! The leg felt warm and supple too. He was alive! He had to be alive!

They'd better make for dry land before the lapping shallows surge into a high tide and drowned them both. He tugged at the fender to lift the car off Pat's leg. The fender snapped off the car as if it were a ten cent plastic model. So much for tough fiber glass bodies. Better lift it by the steel frame. That was all right but he could only raise the car a few inches and tuck the leg out of danger before he had to let it down again. If only he weren't so dizzy. He'd been in a lot better shape the day he'd lifted the car with Dad and Peter Varian and Pat. Maybe he had a concussion? That would make him dizzy. So would shock, though. Better not think about it. He had to get Pat out.

He'd need wedges to jack the buggy up long enough to drag Pat out. Risky to leave Pat long enough to hunt driftwood props, but it was the only chance they had. If only he hadn't passed out. Was that a groan? Mike listened. Nothing. Damn. It must have been the wind whistling under the car. Or the rising water. Had to get started, but if he could bring Pat around it wouldn't be so dangerous to leave.

"Pat! Pat!" Mike called desperately.

"Help. I'm upside down. Mike?"

"I'm here. Don't worry. Man, is it good to hear from you! Undo your seat belt," Mike said.

"Hell, no. I'd fall in the water. Dark under here—get me out, Mike!"

"I'm going after driftwood to prop up the car. I see some real close. Do you know if you're hurt?" Mike didn't like the sound of desperation in Pat's voice. Hysteria. And he was lying about seeing the driftwood. You couldn't see two feet in the pea soup fog. He'd have to stumble over the wood to find it.

"Crushed. Dizzy. Oh, Lord, hurry, hurry, please." The voice faded to a whisper.

And then all was quiet. Mike couldn't get Pat to answer anymore. He must have passed out again. No wonder. Upside down. Be better if he'd snapped off the seat belt. The water wasn't really under the car yet. Maybe if he'd used his own seat belt, the car wouldn't have flipped in the first place? Maybe if he hadn't been thrown clear, they could have righted the car together? Who could tell. Work today and regret tomorrow, Mike reminded himself, as he crawled on all fours feeling for the wood so he wouldn't miss a good piece half covered in sand and fog.

Broken shells and jagged rocks cut into his knees and legs as he crawled along. Beach grass scratched through his wet pants. But bit by bit he carried small finds back to the car, jacking it up a little further with each piece. He forgot everything in collector's triumph when he found a good piece and dragged it back to the car. He was so absorbed that he was surprised to notice when the car was propped almost a foot that Pat had released his belt and was lying on the wet sand. He must have come to. At least he wasn't upside down any more. Mike called again, but it was no use. Still, he was alive if he'd snapped off the belt. At least he had been.

Finally Mike found a railroad tie. That should do it. It took all his strength to drag it back to the car. Then all he had to do was put it in place. If only it didn't topple all the other boards. Would have been more stable on the bottom, but beggars could never be choosers. He'd propped each piece under the car frame as he'd found it so Pat would have breathing space, so he could see light when he came to. Now stay put, Mike pleaded aloud with the railroad tie. It felt stable enough.

"Where could I go?" Pat asked weakly. "What time is it?"

"Lord knows. I don't think it's been long since we crashed. The tide hasn't risen much. But who knows in this fog? Pat, hang on. I'm coming in after you now. Ready?"

"No! Stay there! The car might fall, Mike, and we'd both be pinned. I can make it out. It's just so awful cold, freezing. No use. Can't do it. Damn arm no good. Pull me by the leg, Mike, but stay out there."

Why didn't he stick out his other leg? Obviously because he couldn't, Mike told himself as he inched Pat out slowly. He could feel Pat helping, scrunching along from side to side, like a wounded hermit crab. Finally he caught sight of the fluorescent curly red hair, red even through the fog. One more pull. One more and Pat was clear of the car.

A breaker lapped at Mike's heels and pulled back, scouting for the advancing tide. Like the scout grunion who were followed by millions. They didn't have much time. Pat sounded as if he didn't have much to go on either. Mike knelt and, ever so gently, pulled his brother away from the wreckage of the dune buggy. The next breaker caught Mike in the back and left him shivering. They had just made it.

"We must live right," Pat muttered with a look at the rising tide. Then he passed out.

Mike felt sure he didn't have the strength left to drag Pat or carry him back to the warmth of the first line of dunes. His own legs felt as if they could no longer carry *him*, let alone the dead weight of a solid redhead. Still, there was no choice. Pat was obviously in shock, and shock cases had to be kept warm. One ankle was swollen. There was no chance of keeping a fire going on the beach in the fog and the dampness. It couldn't be more than a hundred yards to the dunes. Besides, they'd be under water in another fifteen minutes if they stayed where they were.

Pat's face looked peaceful, as bland as if he were

sleeping naturally. Mom always said she could remember what lovely babies they were when she saw them sleeping. If only she were here, maybe she'd know what to do. Well, she wasn't here.

Mike hoisted Pat over one shoulder and wondered if he had a concussion. You should never move a concussion case. Just cover him with a blanket and call the doctor. What a joke those First Aid courses were! It was four miles to town and even if he *did* make it and *could* get a doctor, there was a good chance that by the time they got back they'd find rigor mortis had set in. Besides, there was a good chance he had a concussion himself. He was still dizzy.

Their only chance was to build a fire and hope that when they didn't get home for lunch Mom would send out a search party. Thank God she was such a stickler for routine. The tourists would come when the fog lifted and the tide went out—but that was at least four hours away.

Mike tried to keep his mind working on all the possibilities so he didn't have to realize how heavy Pat was. He was bent nearly double under the weight. But he had to look down anyhow to watch out for driftwood, seaweed, and beer cans so he wouldn't stumble. If he once fell, he could never get up again. Never. If only he didn't meet the dead sea lion! He couldn't face that carcass with Pat's fear of the sea in its eyes and its mouth, and its belly pouring out, not again. Surely he'd be able to smell it in time to give the dead animal a wide berth.

He was conscious of the dunes looming ahead, but he did not dare look up, knowing that their very nearness might rob him of the strength he needed to reach their comfort. Besides, his wet feet were numb and, therefore, clumsy, and he had to give all his attention to seeing that they came down securely with each step. The sand was dry and loose and difficult to walk in where they were. There was no danger of drowning if he fell, but Pat might die of exposure.

Finally they came to the first line of dunes. Mike stopped, still carrying Pat. He could not climb thirty feet up in live slipping sand to get over the top of the dune, even without Pat. He would have to skirt around and use whatever protection the gully between the first dunes afforded. It wouldn't be as warm as a cove surrounded by sand walls, but with a fire it should do. It was all he *could* do.

He fell into the lee side of the dune after he rounded the first warm curve of white sand. He fell with Pat across him and could not get up. He didn't know how long he lay like that. He was conscious once of finally being warm, of digging his feet into the sand like a blanket, of hearing the foghorn and the squawk of gulls. He should not have run over that poor gull's clam. It was only when he heard the ocean again and sniffed at the restoring salt air that he realized Pat was lying on top of him and remembered the crash and the green octopus and the urgent need for a fire. God, Pat was heavy. And limp. He must still be out. He was breathing steadily, though. That was good. Should he try to bring him to? Better make a fire first.

Mike crawled out from under his brother and was hit by the cold. Pat must be freezing. Needed a fire. Pat usually had matches. He searched and found some in a pocket, then quickly he covered his brother with sand up to the neck, shoveling it up in great wild handfuls. He'd have had to be more careful if Pat's eyes had been open.

Pat's lips were blue. Did that mean a heart attack? Maybe he should have gone into town for a doctor? How long had it been now? Maybe it had been hours?

The fog was lifting, and he could see enough to spot some firewood without groping around on all fours. That was a break. It didn't help as a clock though. The fog could lift in fifteen minutes. He looked out through the drifts of mist and saw the green dune buggy battered by the tide. The waves broke over its carcass brutally, and Mike wondered if there'd be enough left to warrant hauling it to town. A gull landed on one wheel and stood looking out to sea as if it were the prow of some sailing ship. Maybe the tide would haul the whole car out to sea. Probably not. It would just sink into the wet sand and end up as a john for sea gulls. Stop it. This was no time to get sentimental about a hunk of fiber glass and airplane tires.

Instead, he concentrated on stripping underbrush from the sage and built a tepee of the driest sticks. He found the half burned remains of a previous fire, and then, at the last moment, the wrapper from a loaf of bread and two paper cups. They might make all the difference. Paper caught so easily.

He remembered the driftwood jacking up the car. It would be wet, but once the fire was going it would catch all right. Who knew how long the fire would have to last? He started back to the beach. The beach grass cut his bare feet mercilessly, and once he stumbled over old mattress springs. It was a while before he could get up, but finally he reached the wreckage, and by dashing in between the breakers, he was able to pull most of the wood out, piece by piece, and drag it past the high tide line. He would come back for some of it when he was stronger. He took a few light pieces with him and started back to Pat.

At last he felt ready to light the fire. Miraculously the matches he'd taken from Pat's pocket were still dry. Mike struck the first match. The wind blew it out. He sheltered the second with his hand and the bread wrapper caught. He lit another match. Soon the fire was burning well. He could hardly believe its warmth. Just a little pile of sage twigs and damp sticks.

He was so absorbed in toasting his numb hands that Pat had to call twice.

"Mike, will you please stop crying?" Pat asked in

an exasperated voice.

"Crying?" He put his hand to his face. Sure enough, his cheeks were wet, and he even vaguely remembered sobbing. "Lucky I didn't put out the fire," Mike said sheepishly, drying his eyes on a shirtsleeve.

"Mind bailing me out of this sand cocoon so I can get to that fire?" Pat asked with a grin. "And, by the way, thanks Mike!"

"For what? For half killing you so I could set a speed record?"

"For saving my miserable life," Pat replied firmly. "Now, help bail me out of here. My arm is certainly broken and, unless someone shows up pretty damn soon, you're going to have to set it. We may have to hike into town."

Pat was back in command, and Mike was the little brother again. Mike wanted to say he was sorry and an idiot, but Pat would only say he was a sentimental masochist and wasting good time. For someone who chattered on as he did, Pat was surprisingly difficult to say anything decent to. Mike uncovered him and gently helped him closer to the fire. His ankle was swollen as if he had elephantiasis, and they both knew Pat would never make it four miles to town, but neither mentioned this. Mike used eucalyptus bark strips and his shirt to splint Pat's arm.

"Remember when I was president of the First Aid Club?" Mike asked as he looked at his neat sling with satisfaction.

"Yeah, I remember. And I don't like being a guinea pig any better now than I did then. Dad used to say if we survived your treatment nothing could kill us, and I guess he's right. Matter of fact, he often is.

"Funny, when I thought of getting banged up, I was always deep in the jungles of Asia," Pat ran on, talking now as if he were afraid to stop hearing his own voice. "Won't Paul give me the horselaugh, though? At least this should delay my induction a little while. Do you suppose there might be permanent damage? No. That wouldn't be my kind of luck. Don't mind me, Mike. Every man has his own anesthetic and mine is chatter. My alter ego must be a parakeet. But, seriously, how's the popcorn machine? Maybe we can clean off the salt water. Take it apart piece by piece. Learn the insides of a car like Dad always wanted us to. I knew a guy once who did that and his car ran good as new. Only trouble was that he knew the damn car so well you would have thought he was testing its heartbeat every time you went for a ride. He actually developed a tic from cocking his head to listen. Went to a doctor and guess what he prescribed?"

"A new Corvair and that's how you got your—"

"Very funny! Never mind. You've heard all my jokes. You're too damn smart. But, seriously, we'll do it. We'll start tomorrow—next week, maybe."

Mike thought his car would be sunk to the top of the rollbar by tomorrow, but he grinned and nodded his head. So long as Pat was talking he was O.K., even if the pain took all the color out of his face and the sweat stood out on his forehead. Pat couldn't see himself so the big front worked. Mike cleaned Pat's bruises and cuts as best he could without water while Pat talked on and on about auto crashes his friends had been involved in, how left out he'd felt, and how he could now crash the "in" group with a tale or two of his own. On and on. Talk about diarrhea of the mouth. It would be funny if it weren't so cockeyed noble, considering the pain that showed in his eyes. And so characteristic. Pat had always done the vocal soothing, and he'd always been the one who set the arms. You could call it a division of labor.

Pat's talk darted close to war and how he felt about it and then away again, as if he were afraid Mike might try to get a word in edgewise. Did he think it was his exclusive catastrophe? Did he think it was going to be wiped from the earth forever before Mike reached nineteen? Or was he just too weak and in too much pain to carry on a conversation? Maybe it was easier to talk than to think. Anyway he needn't have worried. Mike had no intention of interrupting. He was too tired. It was easier for him to let this proof of Pat being alive just roll over him in soothing warmth while he watched the fog rise and the tide turn and saw that the fire was fed. If Pat did have a concussion, he shouldn't go to sleep. Maybe he shouldn't talk either? Mike couldn't remember. Who ever thought he'd actually have to use that crazy first aid course, anyhow?

Mike lost all track of time. There was Pat's voice and his injuries and his pain, unspoken and obvious. There was no use in worrying about food unless they had to spend the night. Surely help would come by then. For now, it was better to concentrate on keeping the fire stoked. Dry wood was getting scarcer. He didn't like to go far to gather it because Pat tried to talk louder so he could hear. Maybe Pat was delirious. He certainly wasn't all that coherent. But at least he was still alive. Surely he wouldn't die now?

Sometimes Mike thought he heard the dune buggy cracking up, and he peered out at the tiny green bug in the water. He wanted to run down and check, but if you really thought about it the car was a goner sooner or later, so why upset Pat by running off?

Still, as far as he could tell that strange dry sucking sound, like the pull on a soda straw after you'd reached the bottom of the glass, was only the noise of a receding breaker as it pulled back under the frame and not the sickening crunch of the car itself. Apparently it took a long while to drown a car. Not that there was any hope, really. Still, he couldn't help but root for the little defenseless Meyer Manx standing firm as a rock against the pull of the whole Pacific Ocean. It was going to be hard to tell Mary he'd wrecked the car she hadn't wanted him to have because he might wreck it. Even Peter Varian was bound to remember that he'd taken the car through years of deserts and mountains and come out unscathed only to have it sink in the surf.

Better not think about that either. Concentrate on keeping Pat alive and the fire going. The fire, amazingly successful, might be a beacon as well as security against the fickle sun. Someone might connect the fire on a sunny day with the sinking green overturned car waving its white-walled wheels in the air like a surrender flag. The tide was going down now, leaving a record of its height in a rim of pale yellow froth and rich debris churned from the ocean floor.

Someone should be along soon. It had better be pretty damn soon. Pat would need an ambulance. There had to be time to go five miles back to town and return before the tide came in again. There were some cars far down the beach, scurrying around like brightly colored ants on the tawny sand, but they were taking their own sweet time about moving on. Tourists were notorious for staying close to the pier so they could run for safety with the first big wave. It didn't help, either, that the part of the beach they were on was off limits for clamming. But surely one brave soul, one loner with the soul of a beachcomber or one dune rider, would come down to see what loot the tide had left. It was Saturday, after all. No one was in school. Surely someone would come!

Pat began to doze. As far as Mike could tell, he slept peacefully and naturally. God knew, he needed the rest to cope with the ride back to town. His arm was broken and his left foot or ankle—with the swelling he couldn't tell which—or both? What else? Some internal injury maybe? And on top of everything, he was probably going to get burned to a crisp if they stayed out much longer after being indoors all winter. Mike looked around but there was nothing to make a shelter. Old auto parts washed up from wrecks like theirs today, seaweed, a dead sea lion, mattress springs, but no clothing for either shelter or distress signal.

There must be something. If only he weren't so terribly tired, he'd be able to think of something. He mustn't go to sleep. Had to keep up the fire. Had to watch Pat. All his fault. Might get cold again any time. Sunburn. Four o'clock wind. Hungry. What if no one came? So tired. Awfully sleepy. Funny buzzing.

The buzzing got louder, and Mike fought to open his eyes. Maybe it was an airplane? No. Had the popcorn machine finally sunk? Was that the noise? He looked out, but the green buggy stood like a rock with only tide pool shallows of water around it. It *could* be a motorcycle. He scanned the beach but saw nothing. He was sure he had heard a cycle though, and hoped against hope that Mom had sent Peter Varian out to look for them when they didn't come home for lunch, for the birthday lunch. Birthday. The champagne, still unopened.

Mike stood up and waved wildly. Someone must be

there somewhere. Finally he saw them! It was Peter all right. There was no mistaking that flying white mane or the fire engine red Honda. Thank God! But who was that on the jump seat? Mary? No, it wasn't Mary, Mike decided in some disappointment. It was just some strange man.

"Pat! Wake up, man. Here comes Peter! Peter!"

"God damn, if he doesn't look like Santa Claus," Pat said, propping himself up on his good arm. Wide awake now. "And Dad," he continued softly. "Dad!"

Mike ran down to the beach, stumbling over seaweed, stumbling in the deep sand in his hurry, all the time waving his arms like a windmill. If he could only get to the car. They couldn't miss them if he could only get to the car in time.

"Dad! Dad! Help!" he called.

The motorcycle dug into the wet dirt and upended in a frantic effort to stop, spewing wet sand. The old prospector snapped off the engine and waited impatiently while Dad hopped off before he followed, leaving his cycle sprawling on the beach.

"Thank God, you're alive," Dad said, running toward him.

"Pat O.K.?" Peter Varian asked at the same time.

Mike pointed to the campfire. Peter ran on by him up to the dune. Mike saw the tears in his father's eyes. "I'm sorry, Dad. I took a turn too fast."

"Don't we all," his father answered, and held out his arms.

RIPTIDE

MIKE HALF DOZED in the hospital waiting room. He was getting used to listening only for the sound of the doctor's crepe soles. The shoes caught on the highly polished floor so that each step he made took a little extra effort. At first Mike had thought the doctor's steps were reluctant because they were bringing the final bad news about Pat, but after two days and three nights he realized the hesitation was the same whatever the news and that generally there was no news. It was only the crepe soles.

He and his parents had spent most of the time in

a pale green alcove off the main desk area. Occasionally they went home for a few hours, but mostly they only talked about going home but did not move. Pat had gone into a coma and, after all, no one knew when he might come out and Mom wanted to be there when he did. He had come back just once for a moment when Mike was in his room.

"Put out the incense, Mike," he'd said and then gone back under. There wasn't any incense, of course, but only five bunches of carnations, which made the room smell like a cinnamon stick. He'd thrown them out. Why did people send flowers to a boy, anyway? Probably they wanted to do something and didn't know what else *to* do. That was the whole trouble. There wasn't anything to do. That was the hell of it. All you could do in the world was wait. For a while Mom could cry, but after the first day she was cried out and after that she sat like him and Dad. Three robots.

The hospital routine came and went like a dream. An endless parade of nurses marched back and forth like toy soldiers on a conveyer belt carrying water pitchers and medicines and flowers. No wonder there were so many florists in the world. Pat wasn't the only one with a room full of carnations.

But it was the smells and the sounds of a hospital that got to you. It wasn't so much the little smells of meals or stale cigarettes or even the perfumed sweat of nervous visitors. It was that damn Lysol. If he lived to be a hundred he'd never get over that particular disinfectant. It had gone straight through to the marrow of his bones.

And it wasn't only that. Hospitals were very noisy places in a very hushed way. There were trays banging for what seemed like half a dozen meals a day, wheelchairs squeaking as if no one had ever heard of *Three-in-one* oil, visitors getting the last word in from the doorway to each room, and everybody hushing each other. There was more noise here than between classes at high school. The worse thing, the one that ranked with the Lysol, was the visitor giggle. This was a continuous high pitched yelp like a scared dog, and every visitor seemed to have it. He had even caught himself giggling the last two days. And Dad!

Or maybe this was all just part of the real nightmare that he might miss the doctor with the crepe soled shoes. What was his name? Why would he block out a doctor's name? Pat would know the psychological reasons. He'd have to ask him when he woke up. If he woke up?

He wouldn't think that. Dad said not ever to consider that he might not. The doctor said lots of people with severe concussions went into comas and stayed under longer than two days. It better not be much longer. Mom said that they were to think all the time about Pat getting well, and he'd get the vibrations if they concentrated hard enough. Maybe she was right, and she must be getting through if anyone was; but it was making an old woman of her.

Last time old crepe soles come by he said they'd done a brain probe, which was sticking a long thin needle straight down through the skull and poking around. Anyway, there wasn't anything they could find wrong except some swelling and bruising from the conk on the head Pat got at the time of the accident. Mom and Dad acted as if this was almost the best news in the world, but would they bother a guy in a coma like that unless they thought he'd had it?

And why would the doctor be so especially nice to him if he didn't know he was going to have to face —well, however you cut it and no matter what Dad said about accidents, he'd been driving like a maniac when the car turned over and conked Pat. No one had ever mentioned it, which was a bit creepy. Mom said an accident was an accident. It wouldn't have been so bad if *he'd* gotten the concussion. That would have been logical, too, since he was the one thrown from the car.

Oh, oh, there was old crepe soles again. Hey, he was smiling? Dad jumped up to meet him. If he'd only wait until the doctor reached them, then Mom could hear too. Mom sat as if she couldn't move and he couldn't run off and leave her alone. This time the doctor was coming to them before saying a word. Good guy.

"Mrs. Lamon, I think Pat would like to see you now. He's been conscious about ten minutes and it looks as if he's coming around nicely. At least he says he has a terrible headache." The doctor grinned as if Pat's headache was the most marvelous pain in the world. Maybe it was. At least he knew about it.

"Please, don't ask him any questions," the doctor called after her. She hadn't said a word. Just started crying and trotting toward Pat's room halfway down the hall.

"Is he going to be all right? I mean I know you can't say for sure until you run all those tests, but you must have some idea?" Dad looked as if he was torn between standing there finding out how things really stood and taking off like a rabbit after Mom. The doctor must have thought so, too, because he laid a restraining hand on his shoulder.

"It's probably better if he only sees one person just yet. He feels pretty confused and will for several hours. I asked Mrs. Lamon not to question Pat because he probably can't form answers yet. It's pretty tiring. As for the prognosis, I'd say it's good. We didn't find any evidence of permanent brain damage and, aside from a very slight paralysis of the left side which should clear up in a day or so, he doesn't exhibit any abnormal symptoms. I stayed with him to get some idea before I came out to see you."

"Well, we certainly do thank you, doctor."

"I've mostly just been watching too," the doctor said as he turned back toward Pat's room, his shoes catching on the vinyl tiles as he walked.

"Well, I guess we might as well sit back down and wait for your mother."

"I don't see why the doctor wouldn't let you go in at least. I mean, I wouldn't have minded," Mike grumbled sinking down on the hard wooden captain's chair again.

The next two weeks passed quickly. They spent most of their free time at the hospital, but it wasn't so hard because they could see Pat. Mike and his father drove over together after school every day. Mike was astonished at the patience and gentleness his once explosive Dad showed. He insisted that Mike drive, both to get over his fear of driving and to practice so that he could get his license as a welcome home surprise for Pat. Some surprise. Still, since it seemed to make Dad feel better, he went along with the project. It gave him something to do. He had become the world's jumpiest driver, but Dad kept saying he'd get over that, that over-caution disappeared when you got confidence.

It was still a time of waiting. The paralysis was gone, but the broken foot was not healing properly. Pat was recovering from the concussion so that his headaches were only sporadic, but he might still have a crippled foot. Pat joked that a lame foot would keep him out of the draft, where a concussion would only give him about three month's grace, but he didn't look very happy about it. Finally, the doctor told them the

193

foot would be all right.

"So I come out without a scratch, after all," Pat said, laughing. "Hello, draft board."

"Have you decided what you're going to do about that?" Dad asked.

"Hey, relax, you guys. Pat, you don't have to decide anything while you're flat on your back," Mike exploded. Talk about hounding a man. This was too much.

"So what's to decide, actually. I know I don't want to go in the Army when it means a war I don't understand. On the other hand I'm not cut out to be a Conscientious Objector. Maybe Mike might be. He was always a better swimmer, if you know what I mean, Dad. Shut up just a minute, Mike. It's like being caught in a riptide. Sometimes the best thing is to go along with it just aiming gradually toward shore. You may come in a mile or so down beach, but there you are. I have a little time because of this foot. Maybe I can get another semester in. Who knows, maybe the conk knocked some sense into my head. Maybe I'll turn up all A's." Pat lay back on the pillows exhausted. His white face blended in with the bedding so that only his deep blue eyes and the curly red hair stood out. It took a second to realize how gaunt he was. He'd never broken the scales, but he was really skinny now, as skinny as Mike.

"You'll find a lot of situations in life where that riptide theory of yours holds true," Dad said finally.

Mike personally thought there were plenty of riptides that never let you touch land unless you strug-
gled like hell, but he could see Pat's point and what
was the use of poking holes in his theory?

The next day they went to bring Pat home. It was
already late afternoon when they drove up to the
hospital. The shadow of the building fell over the car
and across the street as Mike pulled to the curb. The
four o'clock wind would be rising soon. At least they
had a sunny day to take Pat home. Almost the first
sunny day since the accident. Must be a good omen.
Mom, Annie, Mary, and Peter Varian, who were
waiting at home for a belated birthday dinner, all said
the sun was a good omen so it must be so.

Mike was too tired to know. Wrung out. It was as
if the day had brought all the time since the accident
into focus *all* over again. And it was overwhelming.
That morning he'd faced the examiners at the Auto-
mobile License Bureau, with its dreary endless gray
maze and its nervous applicants, faced them all a second time and to his great surprise become a licensed
driver. Perhaps because he didn't care? No, that
wasn't quite true. He wouldn't have wanted to put
the car up over the curb again. Especially not the
family Oldsmobile, lent out of kindness or compas-
sion or concern by his father.

But that afternoon he felt dizzy. He could sleep for
a month. There was something extraordinarily pleasant about sitting with the late afternoon sun coming

through the open car windows, something peaceful. Once he and Dad moved into the bustling hospital corridor and took one whiff of that Lysol it would be all over. Still he could not sit there forever. Finally, and with great effort, he checked the emergency brake and pulled the key out of the ignition. As he handed it to his father he noticed that it was a shiny new key. A shiny new key like the one he'd had made for the dune buggy how many lifetimes ago?

"Keep it, Mike. See the *M* on the keychain? You know, Pat's had a key for a year or so. You've got your license. You should have one too," Dad said with a grin.

"But you took a lot for granted. You must have had this made before I even took the test this morning." Mike blushed, grateful for the implied vote of confidence, but knowing he should not mention this. Dad was hard to thank at any time, but impossible when it came to the accident, which he was determined to pretend involved no fault.

"Oh, I have faith once in a while. By the way, the insurance company called this morning. They are willing to total the dune buggy. That means they'll give you the low blue book value which runs about five hundred dollars. Either that or a couple hundred dollars and the car back. They say they can't repair it because it would involve getting all the salt off every piece. I was thinking—"

"Why can't they fix the buggy? It was hardly

196

dented except for the fender I ripped off, and Pat says they can fuse that."

"That isn't the point, Mike. So much salt water got into the motor that it would take a thousand hours to get it all out. Anyhow, if you still want a motorcycle, you could get a pretty decent Honda for five hundred. I think you've enough experience to handle one now."

Mike stared at his father. Three years they'd argued about a motorcycle. For a year they'd hardly been able to talk decently to each other because of a motorcycle. And now, all of a sudden and at the least likely time in the world, Dad was giving him the green light. A green light today didn't mean the old problems between them wouldn't flare up again, though Mike had a feeling they'd never be quite as strong. A good deal of all that was gone. Lord knew quite where or why, but it was gone. Like Dad said, though, that wasn't the point. The point really was that he no longer wanted a motorcycle. It couldn't do one tenth of the things a dune buggy could do. You couldn't ride up the face of a dune on a motorcycle. You couldn't take your girl to a dance or take your brother home from the hospital. A cycle was for loners.

Mike shook his head. "Thanks, Dad. I really mean it. I feel like I'm twenty-one, of age, if you know what I mean. But I don't want a Honda. There's just more I can do with a buggy than a cycle. The choice is something else. Do I want to spend the summer taking the Grasshopper apart and learning what makes it tick putting it back together or do I want to work picking peas and beans so I'll have enough extra to buy another buggy? I don't know. Do you?"

Dad shook his head. "That's up to you. Either way you'll be without wheels for a while."

"I've walked before. All football players should walk. Good for their thigh muscles."

"You can use your new key when your mother and I don't need the Olds. Of course, you'd learn more taking your buggy apart, but there's always the chance it won't *go* back together and then you'd be out the whole shebang."

Mike nodded. How true. He'd have to think about it—later. Not everything had to be done at once. You could drift with a riptide, sometimes. Hell, it looked as if some things were better when you didn't plan. But you couldn't—he shoved the thought away. Right now they were going to bring Pat home.

Mike pushed the front door of the hospital open reluctantly, dreading the noisy hush and the Lysol, and dreading above all that something might have happened to keep them from taking Pat with them. He heard the sound of trays being wheeled through the halls. Time for afternoon temperatures, water change, juice, and medication. Pat would get his last orange juice.

They found him dressed and lying on top of his

198

bed. His foot and his left arm were still in a cast, but his color was good and he'd begun to gain weight. Annie had painted his casts in psychedelic colors.

"Don't they look like rainbows after an earth-quake?" Pat asked proudly, holding up his arm for them to admire.

"Or a technical nightmare."

"Dad, you can do better. That's a grandfather joke," Mike said, laughing.

Pat looked ready to go. His suitcase was standing by the door. What were they waiting for? Did Dad have to check him out first? Maybe he had to see the doctor. Why didn't he get on with it? There was no point staying in this cell block any longer than they had to.

"Well," Dad said after a silence, "we might as well call for the wheelchair and get this show on the road. I can check you out on the way down, Pat. Oh, by the way, this postcard came for you this morning."

Pat reached for the card nervously. Mike thought suddenly that maybe he was in no hurry to leave. It might hurt quite a bit to move.

"Oh, God. Oh, Lord, no. Mike, you'll just never believe this. Lord help the poor Marines!"

"They don't draft you by postcard, do they?"

"Hardly. It's from Trouble. He says to tell the "Sophomore Wonder" to keep up his football. They've made Trouble an MP, Military Police to you, and are shipping him out—to London. He says

199

by this time next month he'll be bouncing other privates from the nightclubs and watching the show for free. Talk about dumb luck."

"There'll be no living with him now."

"To say nothing for International Relations," Dad groaned. He reached up to the bell hanging next to Pat's pillow and rang for the nurse.

"Dad, just one thing. There's a minus tide this afternoon and I was kind of wondering—could we take a run down to the beach? Rent a dune buggy, maybe, and just run down past the accident and back. Revisit the scene of the crime or something. Don't look at me that way. I don't even know *why* but I want to see where it happened. It's all so hazy in my mind."

Mike nodded. So they were going back. Back to see if it were just a strip of beach with dunes on one side and ocean on the other. Back to see it under a sunny sky, to see it in perspective. Half-past four. The wind should be rising along the beach and over the dunes just as it had been when Dad and Peter Varian charged up on their motorcycle the day of the accident. The wind would have blown away all trace of their driftwood fire. They'd have to guess which dune had been their shelter. The sea lion must be badly decayed by now if someone hadn't been appalled enough by the smell to haul it away. And of course, the buggy was gone, reclaimed from the tides by a specially equipped dune tow truck and resting behind Luke's Auto Repair shop.

He hadn't been on the beach since the accident. It was as if the beach and the sea had ceased to exist, and now the memory of salt and sage, of birds skimming white capped ripples over a deep blue afternoon sea, of tawny sand and the clear fresh view of the town and purple mountains beyond the sand and the sea, was overwhelming. Yes, he wanted to go back. He wanted to drive along the beach. Mike grinned.

"Once a beach bum, always a beach bum," he said gently.